"You know, no one is watching us. You don't have to pretend to want to kiss me."

Julian smiled. "If there's one thing I've learned in my years in LA, it's that someone is always watching. But even if there weren't, I would still kiss you."

"Why?" Her dark eyes searched his face in confusion, her brows drawn together.

She honestly didn't think she was kissable. That was a shame.

"It's not that hard. Just take a deep breath, tilt your head up to me and close your eyes."

He intended it to be a quick kiss, knowing it would take a while for them to work up to a convincing one. But he found that once they touched, he didn't want to pull away.

* * *

One Week with the Best Man is part of the Brides and Belles series: Wedding planning is their business...and their pleasure

Dear Reader,

In the first two Brides and Belles books, we were introduced to the designer and jack-of-all-trades Gretchen McAlister. Gretchen has always been more comfortable with her art than with men. She's never considered herself to be the pretty one or the skinny one, and after years without a serious relationship, she has resigned herself to a lonely future with too many cats.

I see a lot of myself—and a lot of many women—in Gretchen. I think most women have struggled with self-esteem issues at one point or another in their lives. We spend so much time focusing on our flaws and comparing ourselves to the unrealistic ideals in magazines and in movies that we can forget how beautiful and amazing each of us is in our own way.

I wanted Gretchen to find a man who truly saw her and everything she had to offer. As a Hollywood heartthrob, Julian was the perfect choice. He's been surrounded by the fake ideals for so long that Gretchen's natural beauty and laid-back lifestyle are a refreshing change. And of course, who doesn't want the chubby girl to end up with the movie star?

If you enjoy Gretchen and Julian's story, tell me by visiting my website at andrealaurence.com, like my fan page on Facebook or follow me on Twitter. I'd love to hear from you!

Enjoy,

Andrea

ONE WEEK WITH
THE BEST MAN

———

ANDREA LAURENCE

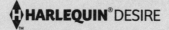

ISBN-13: 978-0-373-73423-8

One Week with the Best Man

Copyright © 2015 by Andrea Laurence

Reclaimed by the Rancher
Copyright © 2015 by Harlequin Books S.A.

The publisher acknowledges Janice Maynard for
her contribution to *Reclaimed by the Rancher*.

Recycling programs
for this product may
not exist in your area.

This edition published by arrangement with Harlequin Books S.A.

For questions and comments about the quality of this book,
please contact us at CustomerService@Harlequin.com.

® and TM are trademarks of Harlequin Enterprises Limited or its
corporate affiliates. Trademarks indicated with ® are registered in the
United States Patent and Trademark Office, the Canadian Intellectual
Property Office and in other countries.

Printed in U.S.A.

H HARLEQUIN®
www.Harlequin.com

CONTENTS

Andrea Laurence is an award-winning author of contemporary romance for Harlequin Desire and paranormal romance for Harlequin Nocturne. She has been a lover of reading and writing stories since she learned to read at a young age. She always dreamed of seeing her work in print and is thrilled to share her special blend of sensuality and dry, sarcastic humor with the world.

A dedicated West Coast girl transplanted into the Deep South, Andrea is working on her own happily-ever-after with her boyfriend and their collection of animals, including a Siberian husky that sheds like nobody's business. If you enjoy her story, tell her by visiting her website, andrealaurence.com; like her fan page on Facebook at facebook.com/authorandrealaurence; or follow her on Twitter, twitter.com/andrea_laurence.

ONE WEEK WITH
THE BEST MAN

Andrea Laurence

To my baby sister Hannah—

Being a girl is tough. Surviving your teenage years with your self-esteem intact is a major feat. You've got a long way to go, but no matter what, I want you to remember: you *are* smart enough, you *are* talented enough and you *are* pretty enough. Don't let anyone tell you otherwise. You can do anything you put your mind to, and if and when you choose to fall in love, that man will be damn lucky to have you in his life. Don't settle for someone that treats you like anything less than the best thing that has ever happened to him.

One

"Pardon me," Natalie said, leaning in toward the man sitting across from her. "Could you run that by us again?"

Gretchen was glad Natalie had said it, because she was pretty darn confused herself. The four owners and operators of From This Moment wedding chapel were seated at the conference room table across from a man wearing an expensive suit and an arrogant attitude she didn't care for. He wasn't from the South; that was for sure. He was also talking nonsense.

Ross Bentley looked just as annoyed with the women's confusion as they were with him. "You advertise From This Moment as a one-stop wedding venue, do you not?"

"Yes," Natalie said, "but usually that means we'll handle the food, the DJ and the flowers. We've never been asked to provide one of the wedding guests a date. This is a wedding chapel, not an escort service."

"Let me explain," Ross said with a greasy smile that Gretchen didn't trust. "This is a very delicate arrangement, so this discussion will need to fall within the confidentiality agreement for the Murray Evans wedding."

Murray Evans was a country music superstar. On his last tour, he'd fallen for his opening act. They were having a multiday wedding event at their facility next weekend, the kind the press salivated over. Those weddings usually required a confidentiality clause so that any leaks about the event are not from the venue. Frankly, Gretchen was getting tired of these big, over-the-top weddings. The money was nice—money was always nice, since she didn't have much—but carefully addressing thousands of invitations in perfect calligraphy wasn't that fun. Nor was dealing with the high-and-mighty wedding guests who came to these kinds of shindigs.

"Of course," Natalie replied.

"I represent Julian Cooper, the actor. He's a longtime friend of Mr. Evans and will be attending the wedding as the best man. I'm not sure how closely you follow celebrity news, but Julian has just had a big public breakup with his costar of *Bombs of Fury,* Bridgette Martin. Bridgette has already been seen out and about with another high-profile actor. As his manager, I feel like it would look bad if Julian attended the wedding alone, but he doesn't need the complication of a real date. We just need a woman to stand in and pretend to be with him throughout the wedding events. I assure you there's nothing inappropriate involved."

Gretchen knew of Julian Cooper—it would be impossible not to—although she'd never seen any of his films. He was the king of dude films—lots of explosions, guns and scripts with holes big enough to drive a truck through them. That wasn't her thing, but a lot of people loved his movies. It seemed a little ridiculous that he would need a fake date. His sweaty, hard abs were plastered all over every billboard and movie preview. While Gretchen might not appreciate his acting skills, she had a hard time discounting that body. If a man who looked like that couldn't get a last-minute date, she was doomed.

"What kind of woman are you wanting?" Bree, their photographer, asked cautiously. "I'm not sure I know many women who would look natural on the arm of a movie star."

"That's understandable," Ross said. "What I'd really prefer is an average woman. We don't want her to look like an escort. I also think it would go over well with Julian's female fan base for him to be seen with an everyday woman. It makes them feel like they have a shot."

Gretchen snorted, and Ross shot a cutting look at her across the table. "We'd be willing to handsomely compensate her for the trouble," he continued. "We're willing to pay ten thousand dollars for the woman's time. Also, I can provide additional funds for salon visits and a clothing allowance."

"Ten thousand dollars?" Gretchen nearly choked. "Are you kidding?"

"No," Ross said. "I'm very serious. Can you provide what we're asking for or not?"

Natalie took a deep breath and nodded. "Yes. We'll make arrangements and have someone in place to meet with Julian when he arrives in Nashville."

"Very good. He flies into Nashville tonight and he's staying at the Hilton." Ross reached into his breast pocket and pulled out a leather wallet. He extracted a handful of cash and pushed it across the table to Natalie. "This should cover the incidentals I discussed. The full payment will be provided after the wedding is over."

Without elaborating, he stood up and walked out of the conference room, leaving the four women in stunned silence.

Finally, Bree reached out and counted the money. "He left two grand. I think that will buy some really nice highlights and a couple fancy outfits, don't you, Amelia?"

Amelia, the caterer and resident fashionista, nodded. "It should. But it really depends on what we have to start with. Who can we possibly get to do this?"

"Not me," Bree insisted. "I'm engaged, and I've got to be able to take all the pictures. You're married and pregnant," she noted.

Amelia ran her hand over her rounded belly. She had just reached twenty-two weeks and found out that she and her husband, Tyler, were having a girl. "Even if I wasn't, I've got to cook for five hundred guests. I'm already in over my head on this one, even with Stella's help."

They both turned to look at Natalie, who was frantically making notes in her tablet. "Don't look at me," she said after noticing them watching her. "I'm the wedding planner. I'll be in headset mode keeping this show on track."

"There's got to be someone we could ask. A friend?" Gretchen pressed. "You grew up in Nashville, Natalie.

Don't you know anyone that wouldn't mind being a movie star's arm candy for a few days?"

"What about you?" Natalie fired back.

"What?" Gretchen nearly shrieked in response to the ridiculous question. They'd obviously lost their minds if they thought that was a viable solution. "Me? With Julian Cooper?"

Natalie shrugged off her surprise. "And why not? He said they wanted a normal, everyday woman."

"Just because he doesn't want a supermodel doesn't mean he wants...*me*. I'm hardly normal. I'm short, I'm fat and never mind the fact that I'm horribly awkward with men. I clam up whenever Bree's musician fiancé comes by. Do you really think I can act normal while the hottest star in Hollywood is whispering in my ear?"

"You're not fat," Amelia chastised. "You're a normal woman. Plenty of guys like their women a little juicy."

Juicy? Gretchen rolled her eyes and flopped back into her chair. She was twenty pounds overweight on a petite frame and had been that way since she was in diapers. Her two sisters were willowy and fragile like their ballerina mother, but Gretchen got their father's solid Russian genes, much to her dismay. Her pants size was in the double digits, and she was in a constant state of baking muffin tops. *Juicy* wasn't the word she would use.

"You guys can't really be serious about this. Even if I wasn't the last woman on earth that he'd date, you forget I work here, too. I'll be busy."

"Not necessarily," Bree countered. "Most of what you do is done in advance."

Gretchen frowned. Bree was right, although she didn't want to admit it. The invitations had gone out months ago. The programs and place cards were done. She would need to decorate the night before, but that didn't preclude her from participating in most of the wedding day activities. "I handle a lot of last-minute things, too, you know. It's not like I'm sitting around every Saturday doing my nails."

"That's not what I'm implying," Bree said.

"Even so, it's ridiculous," Gretchen grumbled. "Julian Cooper? Please."

"You could use the money, Gretchen."

She looked at Amelia and sighed. Yes, Gretchen was broke. They'd all agreed when they started this business that the majority of their profits would go into paying off the mortgage on the facility, so they weren't drawing amazing wages. For Amelia and Bree it didn't matter so much anymore. Bree was engaged to a millionaire record producer, and Amelia was married to a rare jewels dealer. Gretchen was getting by, but there wasn't much left over for life's extras. "Who couldn't?"

"You could go to Italy," Natalie offered.

That made Gretchen groan aloud. They'd found her Achilles' heel without much trouble. She'd had a fantasy of traveling to Italy for years. Since high school. She wanted to spend weeks taking in every detail, every painting of the Renaissance masters. It was a trip well out of her financial reach despite years of trying to save. But Natalie was right. With that cash in her hand she could immediately book a flight and go.

Italy. Florence. Venice. Rome.

She shook off the thoughts of gelato on the Spanish Steps and tried to face reality. "We're overworked. Things are slower around the holidays, but I don't see a three-week Italian vacation in my future. He could give me a million bucks and I wouldn't be able to take off time for a trip."

"We close for a week between Christmas and New Year's. That would cover some of it," Natalie said. "Or you could go later in the spring. If you work ahead with the printing, we can get someone to cover the decorating. What matters is that you'd have the money in hand to go. What can it hurt?"

"Yeah, Gretchen," Bree chimed in. "It's a lot of money, and for what? Clinging to the hard body of Julian Cooper with a loving look in your eyes? Dancing with him at the reception and maybe kissing him for the cameras?"

Gretchen tightened her jaw, choking down another argument, because she knew Bree was right. All she had to do was suck it up for a few days and she could go to Italy. She'd never have another opportunity like this.

"Besides," Bree added, "how bad can faking it with a sexy movie star really be?"

If Ross hadn't been personally responsible for Julian's career success, Julian would throttle him right this second.

"A date? A fake date? Really, Ross?"

"I think it will be good for your image."

Julian sipped his bottled water and leaned against the arm of the chair in his Nashville hotel suite. "Do I look that pathetic and heartbroken over my breakup with Bridgette?"

"Of course not," Ross soothed. "I just want to make sure that her management team doesn't outsmart us. She's already been seen out with Paul Watson. If you don't move on fast enough, you'll get painted as lovesick for her."

"I don't care," Julian exclaimed. "Despite what everyone thinks, I broke up with Bridgette six months ago. We only went out publicly because you insisted on it."

"I didn't insist," Ross protested. "The studio insisted. Your romance was a huge selling point for the film. They couldn't have you two break up before it even came out."

"Yeah, yeah," Julian said dismissively. "If I ever even look twice at one of my costars again, you haul me off and remind me of this moment. But now it's done. I'm over Bridgette and I'm *way* over dating someone just for the cameras."

Ross held up his hands. "It won't be like that. I swear. Besides, it's already done. She'll be here to meet you in about five minutes."

"Ross!" Julian shouted, rising to his full height to intimidate his short, round manager. "You can't just do stuff like this without my permission."

"Yes, I can. It's what you pay me to do. You'll thank me later."

Julian pinched the bridge of his nose between his finger and thumb. "Who is it? Some country music singer? Did you import an actress from Hollywood?"

"No, none of that. They tell me she's one of the employees at the wedding chapel. Just your everyday girl."

"Wait. I thought after what happened with that waitress you didn't want me dating 'regular' women. You said they were a bigger security risk than another star with her own career to protect. You said I needed to stick to women that didn't need my money or my fame." Julian had been dealing strictly with high-and-mighty starlets the past few years at Ross's insistence, but now, a regular girl was okay because he said so?

"I know, and normally that's the case. That waitress just wanted to dig up dirt on you to make a buck with the tabloids. There are a million women just like her in Hollywood. But in this scenario I think it's a smart choice. Women in Nashville are different, and it's an unexpected move. Your female fans will like it, of course, and so will the studios. I've been trying to get you a role as a true romantic lead. This could do it."

Julian didn't really want to be a romantic lead. At least not by Ross's definition. His manager's idea of a romantic film was one where the sexy blonde clings to his half-naked body while he shoots the bad guys. He'd already played that role again and again. When he'd pushed Ross on the topic a second time, he got Julian the "romantic" lead in a movie about male strippers. Not exactly hard-hitting, award-winning stuff. Hell, he'd be thrilled to just do a light romantic comedy. Something without explosions. Or machine guns. Or G-strings.

"I should fire you for this," Julian complained as he dropped down into his chair. It was a hollow threat, and they both knew it. Ross had made Julian's career. He might not be creatively fulfilled by big-budget action films, but the money was ridiculous and Julian needed every penny.

"It will be fine. I promise. It's not a real relationship, so I can break my own rules this once. In a few days, you can go back to Hollywood and date whomever you want."

Somehow, Julian doubted that. Since moving to Hollywood, he hadn't had the best track record with the ladies. The waitress had sold the story of their romance to the newspapers with some other juicy tidbits she'd gotten out of him. The dancer was just looking for a guy to pay for her boob job. So many others were after either his money or his leverage to get into show business.

Ross encouraged him to date other actresses to reduce that issue, but either way, there was usually some kind of confidentiality contract involved. Even with that in place, he'd learned quickly to keep private things private. He didn't talk about his family, his past…anything that he couldn't bear to see in the papers. An after-the-fact lawsuit wouldn't undo the damage once it was out there.

Since his breakup with Bridgette, he hadn't really shown any interest in dating again. It was too damn much work and frankly, just not that fun. How was he supposed to find love when he couldn't even find someone he could trust?

Ross got up from his seat and put his drink on the coffee table. "Well, that should do it."

"Where are you going?"

"I'm leaving," Ross said.

"Leaving? I thought you said my date was on her way over."

"She is. That's why I'm leaving. Three's a crowd, after all. You two need to get to know each other."

Julian's jaw dropped as he watched his manager slip out of the hotel suite. He should've throttled him. He could get a new manager.

With nothing to do but wait, he slumped into his chair and killed time checking his smartphone for missed calls or updates from his family. His mother and brother lived in Louisville, and that was the easiest and most secure way to keep up with them, especially with his brother James's condition. James's attendant usually kept him up to date on how his brother was doing and shared any funny tidbits to make him feel more connected. Today, there were no messages to worry him.

About four minutes later, there was a knock at the door to his suite. His new girlfriend was punctual if nothing else.

Julian got up and went to the door. He looked through the peephole but didn't see anyone there. Confused, he opened his hotel room door wide and realized it was because his guest was very petite. She was maybe five foot two if she had good posture, and she didn't. In addition to being petite, she was curvy, hiding most of her body under an oversize cardigan. She had the look of the average woman on the street, nothing like he was used to seeing around Malibu.

What really caught his attention, however, were her eyes. She had a dark gaze that watched him survey her with a hint of suspicion. It made him wonder what that was about. Shouldn't *he* be suspicious of *her*? Julian had been a part of the Hollywood scene for several years and had seen his fair share of staged relationships. The women were usually attractive and greedy, hoping they might actually charm their fake boyfriend into falling for them so they could take advantage of California's community property laws.

He waited for her to say something, but she just stood there, sort of awkwardly hovering outside his door. "Hi," Julian finally offered to end the silence. "I'm Julian, although you probably already know that. Are you the one the wedding company sent over?"

"Yes." She nodded, her dark brown curls bouncing around her round face. He expected her to say something after that, but she continued to just hover. It made him think that at any moment, she might turn and bolt down the hallway. He was used to his fans being nervous around him, but not skittish. He was certain Ross would blame him if he ran off the woman his manager had so carefully arranged for him.

Julian didn't want a fake girlfriend. He would gladly send this poor woman back home with an apology, but Ross wouldn't have set this up without a good reason. He paid the man to make smart, strategic decisions about his career, so he had to be nice and make this work. Or he'd hear about it.

"And your name is…?" he prompted.

She seemed to snap out of her nervous daze. "Gretchen," she said, holding out her hand. "Gretchen McAlister."

Julian shook her hand, noticing how ice-cold her skin was and how her fingers trembled in his grip. This woman seemed terrified of him. Women usually had a much…warmer reaction to Julian. He had to pry them from his neck and wipe away their lipstick from his cheeks at movie premieres. He needed to warm her up or they were never going to convince anyone—much less a skeptical press—that they were dating.

He took a step back to let her into the hotel room. "Come on in, Gretchen." He shut the door behind them and gestured for her to take a seat in the living room of his suite. "Can I get you something to drink?"

"Something alcoholic would make all this easier," she muttered under her breath.

Julian's lips twisted in amusement as he went over to the minibar. That wasn't a bad idea to help break the ice. At least for her. He didn't drink, but certainly the hotel would've stocked the room with something useful. He wished he *could* drink, but that was on his personal trainer's list of no-no's: no alcohol, no sugar, no carbs, no dairy, no preservatives, no artificial colors, flavors or anything else remotely interesting or tasty.

Unfortunately, he didn't know where to start with a drink for Gretchen. "There's a collection of tiny bottles in here. Feel free to pick whatever you'd like."

Gretchen watched him curiously as she walked over to the bar and pulled out what looked like tequila. He expected her to mix it with something, but instead, watched in surprise as she twisted off the lid and threw back the tiny bottle in a few hard draws. She really must be nervous if she was doing tequila shots just to be in the same room with him.

"You know, you look like you could use one of these yourself. I'm not getting the feeling that you're very happy about this," she said as she looked at him out of the corner of her eye. She tossed the empty bottle into the trash and turned back to sit on the couch. "I know I probably don't meet your standards for a woman you'd date. Mr. Bentley specifically requested an everyday woman, but I assume I'm not what he had in mind. I'm obviously not a Bridgette, so if that's going to be a problem, just say the word and I'll go on my way."

He was doing a crappy job at making her feel welcome. "No, no. I'm sorry," Julian said, sitting down in the chair to face her. "My manager informed me about this whole arrangement literally minutes before you showed up. My reaction has nothing to do with you and the standards you seem to think you fall short of."

"So you're not on board with Mr. Bentley's plan?"

"Not really," he replied. There was no sense in sugarcoating it. "I'll do what I need to do, but this isn't my choice, no. It's pretty common in Hollywood to contract relationships, but that's not my style. I'd rather go to an event alone than with some woman I don't even know. That's probably why Ross sprang this on me—I couldn't get out of it quickly enough. But now, here we are, and I find I'm just not as well prepared as I would like to be."

"Neither am I," she said. "Does one ever really get used to being pimped out by your friends for something like this?"

"Pimped out?" Julian chuckled. The alcohol seemed to loosen her tongue. "That's one way to put it. Welcome to the Hollywood game, Gretchen McAlister. We've all sold ourselves for success. How much did it take for you to toss your good sense out the window and end up on my couch?"

A flicker of irritation crossed her face, blushing her cheeks an attractive pink. It might have just been the tequila kicking in. He'd bet her hands weren't cold any longer. He fought the urge to find a reason to touch her again.

"Apparently, ten grand for my time and another two grand to make me more presentable."

Julian looked over his date of the next few days and frowned. It shouldn't take two thousand to make her presentable, and he hoped Ross hadn't been rude enough to say such a thing. Ross was usually brutally honest, with a set of unrealistic Hollywood ideals. Whereas Gretchen wasn't the kind of woman Julian was normally seen with in LA, she wasn't unattractive. Her skin was creamy and flawless, her lips full and pink. Her eyelashes were so long and thick, he thought they might be fake, but she didn't strike him as that type.

He supposed anyone could use a haircut and a manicure. She could take the rest of the money and buy clothes. Tonight she was dressed as though she'd come straight from her work at the wedding chapel, wearing a plain green shirt and khakis with a brown cardigan, a pair of loafers and argyle socks. Appropriate for winter in the South, he supposed, but not overly dressy. She looked nice. She actually reminded him a lot of his mother when she was younger and life hadn't completely sucked away everything she had.

But instead of complimenting Gretchen the way he knew he should, he went the other direction. He felt himself being drawn in by her shy awkwardness, but Julian had no intention of getting chummy with this woman. She may not be a part of the Hollywood machine, but she'd use him just like everyone else. She was only here because she was being paid a ridiculous amount of money to do it.

"You should've held out for more. Ross would've paid twenty."

Gretchen just shrugged as though the money didn't mean much to her. He knew that couldn't be true. Who would sign up for something like this if it wasn't because they needed the money? He was a millionaire, and he still wouldn't turn down a well-paying role. There was always something he could do with it. Even socking it away in the bank put it to good use.

He doubted that was the case for her, though. She certainly didn't seem to have agreed to this because she was a fan. She was lacking that distinctly starry-eyed gaze he was used to seeing in women. The gaze that flickered over him was appreciative, but reserved. He sensed there was a lot going on in her mind that she wouldn't share with him. He knew he shouldn't care;

she was just a fleeting part of his life this week, but he couldn't help but wonder what was going on under that curly mop of hair.

"Well, now that we've established that I've been had cheaply, do we need to work out any details?"

Yes, Julian thought. It was better to stick to the logistics of the plan. "I came out a few days early to hang out with Murray before the wedding, so you've got some time to buy clothes and do whatever grooming women do. The first event for the wedding is Wednesday night. They're holding a welcome barbecue out at Murray's house. That will be our first official outing. Maybe we should get together here on Wednesday afternoon and spend some time on our story for anyone that asks."

Gretchen nodded. "Okay. I'll get the event schedule from Natalie, the wedding planner. Any special requests?"

Julian's brows went up at her question. "Like what?"

She shrugged. "I've never done this before, but I thought you might have favorite colors for me to wear, or find acrylic nails to be a turnoff, that sort of thing."

He'd never had a woman ask him something like that before. Despite how often people told him they were there for him, they rarely inquired or even cared what he might really want. He had to think about an answer for a moment. "I only have one request, really."

"What's that?"

"Please wear comfortable shoes," Julian said. "I don't know how many events I've sat through where the woman did nothing but complain about her expensive, fancy, painful shoes the whole night."

Gretchen glanced down at her practical and comfortable-looking brown leather loafers. "I don't think that will be a problem. Well, I'll get going." She got up from the couch and held out a card to him.

He accepted it, turning it over to find it was her business card. The design of it was very intricate but delicate, with a shiny ivory damask pattern over a flat white card. The text was in a blush pink, as was an edging of abstract roses, screaming wedding, but not cliché wedding.

"You can reach me at the chapel number during the day or my cell phone the rest of the time. If nothing comes up, I'll see you Wednesday afternoon before the barbecue."

Julian took her hand in his. It was warmer now, and this time, he noticed how soft her skin was against him. He swallowed hard as his palm tingled where their skin touched. His gaze met hers, and he watched her dark eyes widen in surprise for a moment before she pulled her hand away.

"Thanks for doing this, Gretchen," he said, to cover his surprising physical response to her touch. "I'll see you in a few days."

She nodded and bit at her lip as she made her way to the door. After she slipped out, he bolted the lock and turned back to face his room. It suddenly felt more empty and cold than it had when she was here with him.

Perhaps this setup wouldn't be as bad as he thought.

Two

Gretchen felt as if she'd just lived through that make-over montage from the movie *Miss Congeniality*, although it was more painful than funny. Amelia had scheduled her appointments at the day spa they contracted with for bridal sessions, and they were happy to fit in Gretchen for a full day of beauty.

She was expecting a hair trim and some nail polish. Maybe a facial. Gretchen wasn't a movie star, but she didn't think she needed that much work.

Instead, she'd had nearly every hair on her body ripped out. The hair that was left was cut, highlighted and blown into a bouncy but straight bob. Her skin was buffed and polished, her clogged pores "extracted," and then she was wrapped like a mummy to remove toxins, reduce cellulite and squeeze out some water weight. They finished her off with a coat of spray tan to chase away the pastiness. She got a pedicure and solar nails in a classic pink-and-white French manicure that she couldn't chip. They even bleached her teeth.

Thankfully Gretchen didn't have much of an ego, or it would've been decimated. It had taken about seven hours so far, but she thought she might—*might*—be done. She was wrapped in a fluffy robe in the serenity room. Every time someone came through, they took her into another room and exposed her to another treatment, but she couldn't come up with anything else they could possibly do to her.

This time, when the door opened, it was Amelia. If Gretchen's lady parts weren't still tender, she'd leap up and beat her friend with an aromatherapy pillow for putting her through all this. Instead, she sipped her cucumber-infused mineral water and glared at her.

"Don't you look refreshed!" Amelia said.

"Refreshed?" Gretchen just shook her head. "That's exactly the look I was going for after seven hours of beauty rituals. Julian Cooper's new woman looks so well rested!"

"Quit it, you look great."

Gretchen doubted that. There were improvements, but "great" took it a little far. "I should, after all this," she joked. "If this is what the women in Hollywood go through all the time, I'm glad I live way out here in Nashville."

"It wasn't that bad," Amelia said in a chiding tone. "I've had every single treatment that you had today. But now is the fun part!"

"Lunch?" Gretchen perked up.

Amelia placed a thoughtful hand on her round belly.

"No, shopping. They were supposed to feed you lunch as part of the package."

"Yeah, they did. Sort of." The green salad with citrus vinaigrette and berries for dessert hadn't really made a dent in her appetite.

"If you promise not to give me grief while we're shopping, I'll take you out for a nice dinner."

"I want pretzel bites, too," Gretchen countered. "Take it out of my makeover money."

Amelia smiled. "Fair enough. Get dressed and we'll go buy you some clothes and makeup."

"I have makeup," Gretchen complained as she got up, realizing as she spoke that she'd already broken her agreement not to give Amelia grief. It just seemed wasteful.

"I'm sure you do, but we're going to have the lady at the counter come up with a new look for you, then we'll buy the colors she puts together."

In the ladies' locker room, Gretchen changed back into her street clothes, all the while muttering to herself about Italy. It would be worth it, she insisted. *Just think of the Sistine Chapel*, she told herself.

She continued the mantra as the woman at the department store did her makeup. The mantra got louder as Amelia threw clothes at her over the door of the changing room. Gretchen wasn't really into fashion. She bought clothes that were comfortable, not too expensive and relatively flattering to her shape, such as it was.

But as she turned and looked at herself in the mirror for the first time today, something changed. She was still the Gretchen she recognized, but she looked like the best possible version of herself. Those hours in the salon had left her polished and refined, the makeup highlighting and flattering her features. And although she wouldn't admit it readily to Amelia, the clothes looked really nice on her, too.

It was an amazing transformation from how she'd woken up this morning. This department store obviously used fun-house mirrors to make her look thinner.

"I want to see," Amelia complained. "If you don't come out, I'm coming in."

Reluctantly, Gretchen came out of the dressing room in one of the more casual looks. She was wearing a pair of extremely tight skinny jeans, a white cotton top and a black leather jacket. It looked good, but the number of digits on the price tags was scaring her. "I only have two thousand dollars, Amelia. I don't know how much we blew at the spa, but I'm certain I can't afford a three-hundred-dollar leather jacket."

Amelia frowned. "I have a charge account here. They send me a million coupons. We'll have enough money, I promise. You need that jacket."

"I'm going to a wedding. Isn't it more important for me to get a nice dress?"

"Yes, but all the formals are marked down from homecoming, so we'll get one for a good price. You're also going to the welcome party and the rehearsal dinner. You need something casual, something more formal and a few things in between just in case you get roped into the bridal tea or something. And you're going to own this stuff long after this week is over, so it's important to choose good bones for your wardrobe. I like that outfit on you. You're getting it."

"It's too tight," Gretchen complained, and tugged the top away from her stomach. "I'm too heavy to wear clingy stuff like this."

Amelia sighed and rolled her eyes. "I'm sorry, but wearing bulky clothes just makes you look bigger than you are. I wore a 34F bra *before* I got pregnant, okay? I've tried hiding these suckers under baggy sweaters for years, but I wasn't fooling anyone. If you've got it, flaunt it. Well-fitting clothes will actually make you look smaller and showcase your curves."

Gretchen just turned and went back into the dressing room. There was no arguing with her. Instead, she stripped out of the outfit and tried on another. Before they were done, she'd gone through about a dozen other outfits. In the end, they agreed on a paisley wrap dress, a gray sweaterdress with tights, a bright purple cocktail dress, and a strapless formal that looked as if it had been painted with watercolors on the full silky skirt. Gretchen had to admit the gown was pretty, and appropriate for an artist, but she wasn't sure if she could pull any of this off. In the end, she needed to look as though she belonged on the arm of Julian Cooper.

She didn't think there were clothes for any price that would make the two of them make sense. Julian was…the most beautiful man she'd ever seen in person. The movies didn't even do him justice. His eyes were a brilliant shade of robin's-egg blue, fringed in thick brown lashes. His messy chestnut-colored hair had copper highlights that caught the lights and shimmered. His jaw was square and stubble-covered, his skin tan, and when she got close, she could smell the warm scent of his cologne. It was intoxicating.

And that wasn't even touching the subject of his body. His shoulders were a mile wide, narrowing into a thin waist and narrow hips. He'd been wearing an untucked button-down shirt and jeans when they met, but still, little was left to her imagination, they fit so well. The moment he'd opened the door, her ability to perform rational speech was stolen away. She'd felt a surge of desire lick hot at her blushing cheeks. Her knees had softened, making her glad she was wearing sensible flats and not the heels Amelia had nagged her to wear.

When it came down to it, Julian was…a movie star. An honest to God, hard-bodied, big-screen superstar. He was like an alien from another planet. A planet of ridiculously handsome people. And even though she looked pretty good in these expensive clothes with expertly applied makeup, Gretchen was still a chubby wallflower with no business anywhere near a man like him.

Men had always been confusing creatures to Gretchen. Despite years of watching her sisters and friends date, she'd never been very good with the opposite sex. Her lack of confidence was a self-fulfilling prophecy, keeping most guys at arm's length. When a man did approach her, she was horrible at flirting and had no clue if he was hitting on her or just making conversation.

At her age, most women had a couple relationships under their belts, marriages, children… Gretchen hadn't even been naked in front of a man before. On the rare occasion a guy did show interest in her, things always fell apart before it got that far. Her condition seemed to perpetuate itself, making her more unsure and nervous as the years went by.

Being close to any man set her on edge, and a good-looking one made her downright scattered. Julian just had to smile at her and she was a mess. She couldn't find a normal guy to be with her; how would anyone believe a shy, awkward nobody could catch Julian's eye? It was a lost cause, but she couldn't convince anyone of that.

An hour later, they carried their bags out to Amelia's car and settled on having dinner at a restaurant that was a few miles from the mall, near the golf course.

"I'm glad we could have a girls' day out," Amelia said as they went inside. "Tyler had to fly to Antwerp again, and I get lonely in that big house by myself."

Amelia's husband, Tyler, was a jewel and gemstone dealer who regularly traveled the world. They'd hired a woman named Stella to help with catering at From This Moment, so Amelia occasionally got to travel with Tyler, but the further she got in her pregnancy, the less interested she was in long flights. That left her alone in their giant Belle Meade mansion.

"In a few more months, that little girl will get here and you'll never be alone again."

"True. And I need your help to come up with some good names. Tyler is terrible at it." Amelia approached the hostess stand. "Two for dinner, please."

"Good evening, ladies."

Gretchen turned at the sound of a man's voice and found Murray Evans and Julian standing by the entrance behind them. Before she could say anything, Julian approached her and she found herself wrapped in his arms. He smiled at her with a warmth she would never have expected after their awkward first meeting, and he hugged her tight against the hard muscles of his chest.

She stood stiffly in his arms, burying her surprised expression in his neck and waiting for him to back off, but he didn't seem to be in a rush. When he did finally pull away, he didn't let her go. Instead, he dipped his head down and pressed his lips to hers. It was a quick kiss, but it sent a rush down her spine that awakened her every nerve. She almost couldn't grasp what was going on. Julian Cooper was kissing her. Kissing her! In public. She couldn't even enjoy it because she was so freaked out.

He pulled away and leaned down to whisper in her ear. "You need to work on that," he said. Then he wrapped his arm around her shoulders and turned to Amelia with a bright, charming smile.

"What good fortune that we'd run into you tonight. It must be fate. Do you mind if Murray and I join you for dinner?"

"Not at all, please," the redhead said with a smile that matched his own. "Gretchen said the boys would be out and about today, but we didn't expect to run into you down here in Franklin." She had a twinkle of amusement in her eyes that made her seem like the savvy type who knew how to play the game. But judging by the curve of her belly and the rock on her hand, he knew why the redhead had been taken out of the running for his fake girlfriend.

"Excellent." Julian turned to ask the hostess to change the table from two to four, ignoring the woman's stunned expression. He was used to that reaction when he attempted to live a real life outside Hollywood. What bothered him more was the wrinkling of the woman's nose as her gaze shifted to Gretchen in confusion. It made him pull her tighter to his side and plant a kiss in the silky dark strands of hair at the crown of her head.

"What are you two doing out in Franklin?" Gretchen spoke at last, squirming slightly from his arms.

"Well," Murray began, "we wanted to play some golf. Since I live in Brentwood, coming down here to Forrest Hills is easier and we're less likely to run into any photogs."

The hostess gestured for them to follow her to a corner booth in the back of the restaurant. Gretchen slid into one side, and he sat beside her before she could protest. She might not be ready for their ruse to begin, but they were together in public. He hadn't seen any photographers, but one could be around the next corner. The nosy hostess could tip someone off at the local paper. If anyone saw them together, they needed to be playing their parts.

"What are you ladies up to today?" Julian asked after the server took their drink orders.

· "It's makeover day," Gretchen said. "Julian, this is Amelia Dixon. She's the caterer at From This Moment. She's also very fashionable and helped me with my full day of beauty and shopping."

Julian shook Amelia's hand, but he found it hard to turn away from Gretchen once he started really looking at her. She looked almost like a different woman from the one who had shown up at his hotel room the day before. He hadn't even recognized her when they first walked in the restaurant. It wasn't until Murray pointed out that they were the women from the chapel that he realized it was Gretchen. The changes were subtle, a refinement of what was already there, but the overall effect was stunning. She was glowing. Radiant. The straightening of her hair made an amazing difference, highlighting the soft curve of her face.

"Well, she did an excellent job. You look amazing. I can't wait to see what you guys bought for the wedding."

Gretchen watched him with wary eyes, as though she didn't quite believe what he'd said. She'd looked at him that way the first night, too. She was an incredibly suspicious woman. He smiled in an attempt to counteract her suspicion, and that just made her flush. Red mottled her chest and traveled up her throat to her cheeks. It seemed as though she blushed right down to her toes. It was charming after spending time with women too bold to blush and too aware of their own beauty to be swayed by his compliments.

He'd argued with Ross that he didn't think this was going to work after their short, strained meeting, but maybe he was wrong. They just needed to deal with her nerves so her physical reactions to him were more appropriate. She went stiff as a board in his arms, but he had some acting exercises that would help. It was probably fortuitous that they ran into each other tonight. Better they work these issues out now than at an official wedding event.

As the evening went on, it became clear that Julian knew the least about everyone there. Murray had met both women at the various planning sessions leading up to the wedding extravaganza. Julian was starting with a completely clean slate where Gretchen was concerned. Ross hadn't even told him his date's name before they met, and their first conversation hadn't been particularly revealing. They wouldn't just be posing for some pictures this week. They'd have to interact as a couple, and that meant they needed to learn more about each other if they were going to be believable.

"So you said Amelia is the caterer. What do you do, Gretchen?"

Gretchen got an odd look on her face as though she

wasn't quite sure how to describe what she did for a living. It wasn't a very hard question, was it?

"Gretchen is our visual stylist," Amelia said, jumping in to fill the silence.

"I have no idea what that is," Julian admitted.

"Well, that's why I hesitated," Gretchen said. "I do a lot of different things. I design all the paper products, like the invitations and programs. I do all the calligraphy."

"So you designed Murray's invitations?"

A wide smile crossed Gretchen's face for the first time. "I did. I was really excited about that design. I love it when I can incorporate something personal about the couple, and musical notes seemed like the perfect touch."

"They were just what we were looking for," Murray said.

"They were nice. I wouldn't have remembered them otherwise."

"Thank you. I also do a lot of the decorating and work with the various vendors to get the flowers and other touches set up for the wedding and the reception. I'm a jack-of-all-trades, really. On the day of the wedding, I might be doing emergency stitching on a bridesmaid's dress, tracking down a wayward groomsman, helping Amelia in the kitchen…"

"Or pinch-hitting as the best man's date?" Julian said with a chuckle.

"Apparently." She sighed. "I was the only one that could do it."

"You mean, you ladies weren't clamoring over who got to spend time with me? I don't know if I should be insulted or not."

Gretchen shrugged and looked at him with a crooked smile that made him think maybe he should be insulted. "It's got to be better than stitching up a torn bridesmaid's dress, right? It's not so bad to be around me. At least I don't think it is. I'm fun, aren't I, Murray?"

"Absolutely. You're going to have a great time with Julian. Just don't get him talking about his movies. He'll be insufferable."

"What's wrong with my movies?" Julian asked with mock injury in his voice. He didn't really need to ask. He knew better than anyone that all the films he'd done in the past few years were crap.

He'd started out at an acclaimed theater program at the University of Kentucky. He'd gotten a full scholarship out of high school, praised for his senior performance as the lead in *The Music Man*. He'd intended to go on to graduate and do more stage work. Maybe not musicals—he wasn't the best singer—but he enjoyed the acting craft. Then his life fell apart and he had to drop out of school. Desperation drove him to commercial acting, and with a stroke of luck, he ended up where he was now. It wasn't the creative, fulfilling career he'd dreamed of when he was younger, but his paycheck had more zeroes than he'd ever imagined he'd see in his lifetime.

Everyone laughed and they spent a while critiquing the plot of *Bombs of Fury* as their food arrived. The conversation continued on various subjects throughout the evening, flowing easily with the group. Gretchen had been quiet at first, but after talking about her work and mocking his, she started to warm up. Julian actually had a good time, which was rare, considering he was having to eat salmon and steamed broccoli while the rest of them were enjoying tastier foods. It should be against the law to be in the South and not be able to eat anything fried.

When it was over, they headed out to their cars as a group. He walked Gretchen to the passenger door of Amelia's SUV and leaned in close to her. "I had fun tonight."

"Yeah," she said, nervously eyeing him as he got close to her. "It was a pleasant surprise to run into you."

"I guess I'll see you tomorrow afternoon." Tomorrow was the welcome party and their first official time out as a couple.

"Okay. Good night."

"Good night." On reflex, Julian leaned in to give her a kiss good-night. He was stopped short by Gretchen's hand pressed against his chest.

"You know, no one is watching us. You don't have to pretend to want to kiss me."

Julian smiled. "If there's one thing I've learned in my years in LA, it's that someone is always watching. But even then, I would still kiss you."

"Why?" Her dark eyes searched his face in confusion, her brows drawn together.

She honestly didn't think she was kissable. That was a shame. She was very kissable, with pouty lips glistening from just a touch of sparkly lip gloss. If he were interested in that sort of thing. Tonight, however, he was more focused on their cover and getting it right.

"I'm going to kiss you again because you need the practice. Every time I touch you, you stiffen up. You've got to relax. If it means I have to constantly paw at you and kiss you until you loosen up, so be it." He'd had worse assignments.

Gretchen bit her bottom lip. "I'm sorry. I'm just not used to being touched."

He wrapped his hand around hers and pulled it away from his chest, where she'd still been holding him back. "It's not that hard. Just take a deep breath, tilt your head up to me and close your eyes."

She did as she was instructed, leaning into him like a teenage girl being kissed for the first time. He shook away those thoughts and pressed his lips against hers. He'd intended it to be a quick kiss, knowing it would take a while for them to work up to a convincing one. But he found that once they touched, he didn't want to pull away.

Gretchen smelled like berries. Her lips were soft, despite the hesitation in them. A tingle ran down his spine, the kind that made him want to wrap his arms around her and pull her soft body flush against his hard one. He settled for placing a hand on her upper arm.

She tensed immediately, and in an instant, the connection was severed. He pulled away and looked down at her, standing there with her eyes still closed.

"You did better this time," he noted.

Her dark lashes fluttered as her eyes opened. A pink flush rushed across her cheeks as she looked up at him with glassy eyes. "Practice makes perfect, I guess."

He laughed softly. It certainly did. "I'll see you tomorrow afternoon. Be sure to bring extra lipstick."

"Why?" she asked, her brow furrowed.

Julian smiled wide and took a step back toward where Murray was waiting for him. "Because I plan to remove all of it several times."

Three

Gretchen made her way back up to Julian's hotel suite the next day. This afternoon, she wasn't as nervous as her first visit, but she still had butterflies in her stomach. She was pretty certain that last night's kiss had something to do with it. She'd been kissed by only four men before last night, and none of them had been movie stars.

She couldn't even sleep last night. His threat to remove her lipstick several times over lingered in her mind. He was going to kiss her again. She felt a girlish thrill run through her every time the thought crossed her mind, quickly followed by the dull ache of dread in her stomach.

There was nothing she could do about it, though. She had to live through this. It was only four days. She could make it through four days of almost anything. She knocked at his hotel room door and waited, anxiously tugging at her paisley wrap dress.

"Hey, Gretchen," Julian said as he peeked around the door with a head of damp hair. "You'll have to excuse me—I was running late. Come on in. I've just got to finish getting dressed."

He stepped back and opened the door wider. As Gretchen entered the suite, she realized he'd been hiding his half-naked body behind the door. Just his hair wasn't wet; all of him was. He had a bath towel slung low around his waist, but otherwise, he was very naked.

She didn't even know what to say. As he closed the door behind her, all she could do was stare at the hard, tanned muscles she'd seen in the movies and on advertisements. His body didn't even look real, although she could reach out and touch it. It was as if he was Photoshopped.

"Gretchen?"

She snapped her head up to see Julian watching her with amusement curling his lips into a smile. She could feel the blood rush hot into her cheeks when she realized she'd been caught. "Yes?" she said.

"Go ahead and grab a seat. I'll be right back."

"Yeah, okay."

Turning as quickly as she could, she focused on the couch, gluing her eyes to the furniture so they couldn't stray back to Julian's naked, wet body.

He disappeared, thankfully, into the bedroom. The moment the door closed, she felt the air rush out of her lungs. Sweet Jesus, she thought as her face dropped into her hands. She was about as smooth as chunky peanut butter. There was no doubt that Gretchen was miserably in over her head. There had to be a better person to do this than her.

"Sorry about that," he said as he came out a few minutes later. He was wearing a pair of charcoal dress pants and a navy dress shirt that made his eyes seem as if they were an even brighter blue. "I didn't want to leave you out in the hallway while I got dressed. I hope that was okay."

"It's fine," she said dismissively. Hopefully convincingly. "It's not like you don't run around like that in half your movies anyway. Nothing I haven't seen."

He chuckled as he settled down on the couch beside her. "Yeah, most of my modesty went out the window a few years ago. Once you film a sex scene with thirty-five people watching, then millions watch it on the big screen, there's not much left to worry about."

"Do you do a lot of sex scenes?" Gretchen asked. She couldn't imagine how invasive that would be. She couldn't even work up the courage to take her clothes off in front of one man, much less a roomful.

"There's usually one in every film. I typically save the female lead from the bad guy and she thanks me with her body. It's always seemed a little cliché and stupid to me. You'd think someone would be too traumatized for something like that, but apparently I'm so handsome, they can't help themselves."

"I'm sure most women in real life couldn't help themselves either. You're in…excellent shape."

He grinned wide, exposing the bright smile that charmed women everywhere. "Thank you. I work very hard to look like this, so it's nice to be appreciated."

"I can't imagine what it would take."

"I can tell you. I do high-intensity interval training four days a week and run about ten miles a day the other three. I have given up all my vices, and my trainer has me eating nothing but lean protein, vegetables and some fruits."

Gretchen's eyes grew larger the more he talked. That sounded miserable. No pizza, no bread, no cookies. He looked good, but what a price. "I, obviously, am not willing to put that much work in."

"Most people aren't, but I make my living with these abs. It's not exactly what I'd planned when I moved to California, but it's worked out. Even then, there are days where I'd kill for a chocolate chip cookie. Just one."

That just seemed sad. She was no poster child for moderation, but there had to be some middle ground. "I guess the wedding cake is out, then. That's a shame. Amelia does amazing work."

Julian narrowed his gaze at her. "Maybe I'll make an exception for a bite or two of her amazing cake. I'll let you feed me some of yours so I'm not too tempted."

She couldn't even imagine feeding Julian cake while they sat together at the reception. That seemed so intimate, so beyond where they were together. She knew nothing about him, aside from the fact that he was out of her league.

"I need to tell you something," she said. The words shot out of her mouth before she could stop them.

His dark brows went up curiously. "What's that?"

"It may be painfully obvious to you, but I'm not very good with this kind of thing. I haven't been in many relationships, so this whole situation is alien to me. I don't know if coaching will be enough for me to pull this off." She stopped talking and waited in the silence for him to put an end to this torture and terminate the relationship agreement. If they hurried, maybe they could find a more suitable replacement before the welcome dinner. Anyone would be better than Gretchen.

"I think that's charming," he said with a disarming smile. "Most of the women I know mastered flirting in kindergarten. But no worries. I'll teach you what you need to know."

"How can you teach me how to have a relationship in only a few hours if I haven't mastered it in almost twenty-nine years?"

He leaned in and fixed his bright blue gaze on her. "I happen to be an actor," he confided in a low voice. "A classically trained one at that. I can teach you some tricks to get through it."

Tricks? How could a few acting drills undo fifteen years of awkwardness around men? "Like what?"

"Like reframing the scene in your mind. For one thing, you've got to stop thinking about who I am. That's not going to help you relax. I want you to look at the next few days like a play. You and I are the leads. I'm no more famous than you are. We're equals."

"That's a nice idea, but—"

Julian held up his hand to silence her. "No buts. We're actors. You are a beautiful actress playing the role of my girlfriend. You're meant to be here with me and you're perfectly comfortable with me touching you. That's how it's supposed to be."

Gretchen sighed. It would take more than a little role-playing for her to convince herself of that. "I'm not a beautiful actress. I can't be."

"And why not?" He frowned at her, obviously irritated by her stubbornness to play his game.

"To be a beautiful actress, one must first be beautiful. Only then are acting skills relevant."

Julian narrowed his gaze at her. She squirmed under the scrutiny. They both knew she wasn't Hollywood starlet material; there wasn't any need to look so closely and pick apart the details of her failures.

He reached out and took her hand in his. "Did you know that Bridgette has a mustache she has to get waxed off? She's also not really a blonde, and most of her hair is made up of extensions. Her breasts are fake. Her nose is fake. Everything about her is fake."

"And she looks good." The money was well invested in her career if what he said was true. If Gretchen had a couple grand just lying around, she might make a few improvements herself.

"Julia Monroe is legally blind when she isn't wearing her contact lenses. If her makeup artist doesn't contour her face just right, she looks like a guy after a losing boxing match."

Julia Monroe was one of the biggest and most sought-out actresses in Hollywood. Gretchen had a hard time believing she could look anything but stunning.

"Rochelle Voight has the longest nose hairs I've ever seen on a woman, and her breath is always rancid. I think it's because all she ever eats or drinks are those green juices. I hate when I have to kiss her or film close scenes."

Was he serious? "Why are you telling me all this?"

"Because you need to know that it's all an illusion. Every single one of the Hollywood beautiful people you've compared yourself to is a carefully crafted character designed just for the cameras. We're far from perfect, and more than a few of us couldn't even be described as beautiful without our makeup and hair teams."

"You're telling me everyone in Hollywood is secretly ugly, so I shouldn't feel bad."

He smirked and leaned in to drive home his point. "I'm saying you're an attractive woman—a realistically attractive woman. You shouldn't put yourself through the wringer comparing yourself to an unrealistic ideal. It's all fake."

Gretchen's brows went up in surprise. Even with her makeover, she felt as if Julian were only tolerating her because he couldn't get out of the arrangement. Could he actually believe what he said, or was he just trying to boost her ego enough to get them through this week together?

"Everything about me is fake, too," he said.

It was easy to believe the women he'd spoken about were painted to perfection, but everything on Julian looked pretty darn real to her. "Come on," she chided, pulling her hand from his. She knew he was putting her on now.

"No, I'm serious. These baby blue eyes are colored contacts. The highlights in my hair are fake. My teeth are porcelain veneers because my parents couldn't afford braces when I was younger. My tan is sprayed on weekly. Even my accent is fake."

"You don't have an accent," she argued.

"Exactly. I'm from Kentucky," he said with an unmistakable twang he'd suppressed earlier. "I have an accent, but you're never going to hear it from me because I hide it like everything else."

Gretchen sat back against the cushions of the couch

and tried to absorb everything he was telling her. It was a lot to take in all at once.

"We may all have fake hair and wear makeup and put ourselves through all sorts of abuses to chase the elusive beauty and youth, but we're all actors. This is just our costume. So think of your new makeover as your costume. You've been given all the tools you need. Are you ready to play the role of Julian Cooper's girlfriend?"

She took a deep breath and straightened up in her seat. "I think so."

He cocked his head to the side and lifted a brow at her in challenge.

"I *am*," she corrected with faux confidence in her voice. "Let's do this. Where do we start?"

Julian smiled and turned to face her on the couch. "Okay. When I was in acting school, one of my professors was adamant about throwing the hardest scenes at us first. He didn't let us warm up or start with a less challenging part. We had to open with the dramatic soliloquy. His theory was that once you did that, everything else would come easier. So we're going to start with the hardest part of your role."

Gretchen tensed beside him. The hardest part? It all seemed pretty challenging. She'd be much happier working her way up to the comfort level she needed to pull this off. "How are you—"

He lunged forward and pressed his lips to hers, stealing the question from her lips. Unlike their quick, passionless pecks at the restaurant the night before, this kiss packed a punch. Julian leaned into her, coaxing her mouth open and probing her with his tongue.

She wanted to pull away, but he wouldn't let her. One of his hands was at her waist and the other on her shoulder, keeping her from retreating. Closing her eyes, she remembered she was an actress playing a part. She stopped fighting it and tried to relax. Maybe she could let herself enjoy it for once.

When her tongue tentatively grazed along his, he moaned low against her mouth. The sound sent a shock wave of need through her body making her extremities tingle. She wrapped her arms around his neck and pulled him closer to her. When she'd relaxed against him, his grip on her lessened and his hands became softer and exploratory. They slid across the silky fabric of her dress, finally coming to rest as they wrapped around her waist.

Just when Gretchen had relaxed into his arms and was enjoying their experimental kiss, she felt him tug hard against her. Mercy, but he was strong. Those muscles weren't just for show. The next thing she knew, she was in Julian's lap, straddling him. Her dress rode up high on her thighs and she could feel the warm press of his arousal against her leg.

She almost didn't believe it at first. Gretchen hadn't felt many erections in her time. She hadn't anticipated feeling one here, for sure. Could Julian really be turned on by their kiss, or was he just a very convincing actor? The concerning question startled her enough to make her break away from the kiss. The second her eyes opened, she regretted it. In the moment, things had felt right. Exhilarating and scary, but right. Once she pulled away, all she could do was look awkwardly at the man in whose lap she was sitting. It was a decidedly unladylike and bold place to be, and she wasn't comfortable with either of those adjectives. She could feel the heat in her chest and throat and knew she was blushing crimson in her predicament.

Julian didn't seem to mind. Their awkward parting and her extra pounds in his lap were irrelevant if the pleased grin on his face told her anything. She couldn't tell if he was happy she was doing so well, if he was that good an actor, or if he really was having a good time with it.

"Excellent work," he said. "You're an A pupil."

"Does that mean I should get off your lap so we can move on to the next lesson?"

He shook his head and wrapped his arms tighter around her waist. "Not a chance. Just because you're a quick study doesn't mean you don't need the lessons. We're going to work on this a little more."

"How much more?"

"We're going to sit on this couch and make out until it feels like the most natural thing in the world for us both. If you're going to fool the cameras, we can't stop short of anything less than authenticity."

Gretchen swallowed a chortle of laughter. She wasn't sure that making out with a man like him would ever feel natural, but she wasn't about to complain any time soon about extra lessons.

Julian's rental car was only a few miles from Murray's house, where they were hosting the welcome barbecue. Julian had spent a good part of the past hour going over their manufactured backstory with Gretchen.

"Okay, tell me again how we met. People are going to ask."

She sighed and turned to look out the passenger side window. "You came out here to visit Murray a few weeks ago and happened to join him on a trip to the venue, where you met me. We hit it off, you asked me out for a drink. We've been texting and talking since you went back to LA, and you came back to Nashville early for us to spend time together."

She nailed it. He knew she would. Beneath that shy buffer, Gretchen was one of the smartest, funniest women he'd ever met. It just took a while to get through the nerves. She could handle this; she just couldn't let her anxiety get in the way. "Have we slept together yet?"

Gretchen looked at him with wide eyes. "No, I doubt it. I think we may have traded some saucy texts, but I'm making you wait a little while longer."

"You're a little minx. Good to know."

Julian slowly pulled the car into the driveway and stopped at the large wrought-iron fence, where a small crowd of camera-toting men and fans were loitering. "Smile, you're on *Candid Camera*."

"What do I do?" she asked.

"Just pretend they aren't there. That's the easiest thing to do. Maybe play it up for them a little bit." He reached out and took her hand, holding it in an effortless way as they waited for security to open the gates. Once they pulled through there, they followed the circular driveway to the house, where a valet was waiting. He left the keys in the ignition and turned to look at her. "Any last questions before we do this?"

"Who knows the truth about us?"

That was a good question. "Murray, obviously. And I'm sure he told his fiancée, Kelly. That should be it since Ross won't be at the festivities. Everyone else here thinks you're my new girl."

She nodded and took a deep breath. "Let's get our party on, shall we?"

The valet opened her door and she stepped out, waiting for Julian to walk around and meet her. Together, they walked up the stairs to the front door. When the massive oak doors swung open, they were bombarded with a cacophony of sounds and delicious smells. Murray had spared no expense with even the smallest of events. There were easily a hundred people throughout the large open areas of the ground floor and more outside on the heated deck. A bluegrass band was playing in the gazebo in the backyard, and parked out there was a barbecue truck, smoking ribs and brisket for everyone.

There was a large bar set up in the dining room, just past the buffet of goodies that he knew was only to hold people over until the main course was ready. Shame he couldn't eat any of it.

"Would you like a drink?" he asked, leaning down to murmur in her ear.

"Please."

They went over to the bar, where he got her a margarita on the rocks and got himself sparkling water with a twist of lime. They had a huge keg of beer from a local Nashville microbrewery, which he'd love, but he knew he shouldn't. There would be enough temptations this week without starting off on the wrong foot. As it was, he hadn't worked out since he got here.

"So you don't drink?" Gretchen asked. "Is that a health thing or a moralistic thing?"

"Health. Too many empty calories. One too many beers and all my dietary rules will go out the window. You don't want to find me passed out in a half-eaten pizza, I assure you."

"Scandalous!" she mocked.

"I know, right?" He looked around and spied Murray and Kelly out on the patio. "Have you met Kelly?"

"The bride? Yes. She's been to the facility several times going over details."

"Okay, good. Let's go say hi to the happy couple, then we can find a comfortable place to hang out and hide from most everyone."

"You don't have friends here?"

Julian shook his head. "Not really. Murray and I were roommates in college. When I dropped out and moved to LA, we kept in touch, but I don't really know any of his Nashville friends. I'm mostly here for moral support."

They stepped out onto the deck and greeted the engaged couple.

"So, this is the new lady Murray has told me so much about," Kelly said with a wide smile and a twinkle in her green eyes. "It's good to see you outside of work, Gretchen. I have gotten so many compliments on the invitations. I can't wait to see what you've got in store for the wedding. I think the programs are going to be fabulous."

"Thank you," Gretchen said with a smile.

Julian watched the two women as they chatted about wedding details. From that night at the restaurant, Julian had noticed that Gretchen's reluctance faded away when she talked about her work. She was like a totally different person. She nearly radiated with a confidence that vanished the moment the attention shifted from her art back to her. He understood that. He'd much rather talk about his films, such as they were, than talk about his family or his upbringing. Those were tales better left untold.

"Do you mind if I steal her away?" Kelly asked. "I want to introduce her to my bridesmaids."

"Sure." Julian bent down and planted a kiss in the hollow just below her ear. She shivered but didn't pull away or tense up. Bravo. "Hurry back."

Gretchen gave him a wave and disappeared into the house with Kelly.

"How's that going?" Murray asked.

"Better than expected. I've got her loosened up, so that's helped."

"You're doing a good job, whatever it is. When you came out on the patio together, there wasn't a question in my mind that you two were a couple."

"Really?" Julian smiled. He was pleased they'd come so far, so quickly. Perhaps he wouldn't have to deal with Ross's sour disposition later in the week if this worked out. "I am an award-winning actor, you know."

"The golden popcorn statuette from MTV for Best Fight Scene doesn't really stack up to a Screen Actors Guild Award."

"Don't I know it," Julian grumbled. One day, he wanted a real award for a movie with substance. Once he'd told Ross he wanted to do a movie with depth and the next thing he knew, he was in a movie about terrorists who take over a submarine. Just another flick where he lost his shirt eventually.

"It didn't look like acting to me," Murray said. "You two really look like you've got some chemistry between you. Real chemistry. I'm surprised. She didn't strike me as your type, but stranger things have happened. I, for one, never thought I'd end up with my opening act."

Julian listened to his friend and thoughtfully sipped his drink. He was right. There was something building between them. He didn't know what it was—novelty perhaps. Gretchen was nothing like any of the women he'd ever dated before, and it wasn't just physical differences.

For one thing, she wasn't a vain peacock of a woman. Julian spent his fair share of time in the hair and makeup trailer during films and for official appearances, but it was always a fraction of the time his female costars put in. He got the feeling that Gretchen's day at the spa was a rarity for her. She took care of herself, but her whole self-worth was not wrapped up in her appearance. She was a skilled artist, a savvy businesswoman, and that was more important to her than clothing designers and a close, personal relationship with her colorist.

She also didn't seem that impressed by him. Gretchen was nervous, to be sure, but he got the feeling she was that way around most men. She was aware of his celebrity status, but he couldn't tell if it just didn't impress her, or she didn't care for his body of work. He'd been greeted by plenty of screaming, crying women on the verge of passing out when he touched them. If Gretchen passed out at his touch, it was probably because she'd tensed up and locked her knees.

It had been a long time since he'd been around a woman who didn't care about his money or what he could do for her. She didn't secretly want to act. He wasn't aware of her carrying around a screenplay in her purse for him to read and pass on to a producer. Gretchen was real. She was the first authentic woman he'd spent time with in a really long while. He'd been in California so long, he'd forgotten what it was like to be with a woman instead of a character.

He turned and glanced through the wall of French doors into the house. He spied Gretchen and Kelly standing by the buffet chatting with another woman. Gretchen was smiling awkwardly, carrying on the conversation as best she could. He knew the exact moment the discussion shifted to her work, because she lit up like the sun. She might not think she was a beautiful woman, but he'd never seen anyone more radiant in that moment.

Gretchen was slowly drawing him in. He never intended to let himself get that close to his fake date, but he couldn't help it. He fought the urge to text his brother and tell him about her. James always loved it when his aide would relay stories about Julian's escapades, and he thought his brother would take to Gretchen. She was a talented artist with a quick wit and coy smile. She seemed to enjoy the pleasures in life, drinking her margarita and nibbling on goodies without remorse. She knew who she was, and she lived the life she wanted to.

It was an attractive quality that made him both extremely jealous of her and desperate to have her all at once.

Four

Gretchen crept quietly into the office Thursday morning. She didn't have any wedding-related activities with Julian today, so she wanted to get some things set up for the weekend. Despite the assurances from her coworkers that she didn't have much to do the day of the event, there was plenty that needed to be organized beforehand. And the more she could get done without her coworkers knowing she was there, the better. She wasn't ready for the inquisition.

"Look at you," a woman's voice called down the hallway just before Gretchen reached her office. "Creeping around in the hopes we wouldn't see you. Your hair might be different, but we can still recognize you, you know."

Turning around, Gretchen saw Bree standing outside her office. There was a knowing smirk on her face, and her arms were crossed over her chest.

"Morning, Bree," Gretchen tried to say brightly.

"Don't 'morning' me. You go ahead and get settled, but you'd better know we want to hear all about it."

With a sigh, Gretchen nodded and continued into her office. She hoped it would be quick. They did have a huge, expensive wedding this weekend. Amelia, especially, didn't have time to waste with all those people to feed.

Setting down her things, Gretchen didn't even bother getting on her computer. Instead, she went to the door that led to her storage area. She scanned the various box labels on the shelves, finally identifying the box with the Murray wedding paper goods.

She put it on her desk and lifted the lid. Inside were the wedding programs she'd had printed weeks ago. Beside them were the name cards, table markers and menus. Gretchen had thoroughly gone over everything when they arrived, so she knew they were good to go. She carried the programs into the chapel and left them on the small table just inside. The name cards were left on the round table outside the reception hall. Once the table linens were put out and the centerpieces placed, the cards would be laid out alphabetically for attendees to find their table assignment.

Gretchen continued on through the glass double doors into the reception hall. The large, open room was just a shell of what it would be. The bones were there—sparkling chandeliers and long draped panels of white fabric were hanging overhead, the stage and the dance floor cleared and ready to be occupied by tipsy revelers. The cleaning crew had already been through the day before to vacuum and arrange the tables and chairs.

It would take hours of work to decorate the room. She

hoped to get a head start on some of it today, although a lot of things were last-minute, such as the dishes and the floral arrangements. The wedding was black and white, following along the musical note theme, so the dry cleaning company would deliver their cleaned, pressed white and black table linens sometime this morning. Some custom hand-beaded sheer overlays were ordered to be put over them, making the white tables look like sheet music. The napkins needed to be folded. Several hundred white pillar candles had to be put out.

Gretchen nervously eyed the bare ballroom. The list of things she had to do was staggering. How had she allowed herself to get roped into this romance charade? Just because things were handled the day of the wedding didn't mean she wasn't running around like a chicken with its head cut off the days leading up to it.

"Gretchen, the dry cleaning delivery is here." Natalie stuck her head into the ballroom. She was wearing her headset, as usual, as she was constantly on the phone. She was the command center of the entire operation, coordinating vendors, talking to clients, booking future events and managing the bookkeeping.

"Awesome, thank you."

She helped unload all their clean linens into the ballroom and decided she wanted to start laying them out. She didn't have time to waste.

"I'm ready to hear about yesterday." Amelia walked into the ballroom with Bree on her heels. "My cakes are cooling and I've got some downtime."

Downtime? Gretchen tried not to snort. "Well, I don't have downtime, so if you want to hear about yesterday, you can listen while you help me drape all the tables."

"Fair enough." Bree shrugged. She reached for a tablecloth and flung it over the nearest table.

"We're alternating black and white," Gretchen explained, and they all started at it. They got through about a third of the tables before Bree gently reminded her that they weren't helping out of the goodness of their hearts.

"So, spill it. Did you kiss him?"

Gretchen felt her cheeks turn crimson again. "Yes. I kissed him a lot. He insisted we kiss until I could relax while I was doing it."

"That is just crazy," Bree said. "You're getting paid to make out with Julian Cooper. How did this even happen?"

Shaking her head, Gretchen covered another table in black linen. "I recall you all twisting my arm until I agreed to it."

"Are you getting more comfortable?" Amelia asked, ignoring Gretchen's pointed accusation.

"Yes. I think we're finally to the point where people might actually believe we know each other."

"Biblically?"

"Ugh," Gretchen groaned. "I haven't known anyone biblically, so I can't really say."

"Say what?" Bree stared her down, the linen in her hands pooling on the table. "Did you just say what I thought you said?"

Amelia narrowed her gaze at Gretchen, too. She should've kept her mouth shut about the whole thing. She'd gotten good at it after all these years, even keeping the truth from her best friends. Now the cat was out of the bag.

Gretchen straightened the cloth on the table and admitted the truth, reluctantly. "Yep."

"You're a virgin?" Bree nearly shouted. "How could we not know that you're a virgin?"

"Hush!" Gretchen hissed. "Don't shout it across the ballroom like that."

"I'm sorry," she said, her blue eyes as big as saucers. "It just never occurred to me that my twenty-nine-year-old friend was keeping a secret that big. Did you know?" Bree turned to Amelia.

"I did not."

"You didn't tell any of us?"

"She told me," Natalie said, coming into the room. "It's been a long time, but I haven't gotten any updates that would lead me to believe things had changed."

That was true. Natalie was the only one she'd told, and that had been on a long-ago college night where they'd stayed up late studying, ended up getting into a cheap bottle of wine and spilled their secrets to each other. Natalie was the right person to tell. She wasn't a hopeless romantic like Amelia or pushy like Bree. She took the knowledge at face value and didn't press Gretchen about it.

Bree dropped the tablecloth and sat down in the chair. "Stop, everyone, stop. You all sit down right now and tell me what the heck is going on. How could you keep that from us? And why would you tell Natalie, of all people?"

"Hey!" Natalie complained.

Gretchen frowned at Bree and dropped into a nearby chair. "Bree, how could you not tell us that Ian was your ex before you went up into the mountains to take his engagement photos?"

Bree's nose wrinkled, and she bit at her bottom lip. "It wasn't relevant at the time."

"And neither is my sexual inexperience."

"It might not be relevant to running the business, but as your friend, it seems like something we should've known."

"Known what? That I'm so incredibly awkward with men that I've driven them away since I was fourteen? That my self-esteem is so low that I can't believe a guy could really be interested in me and I look suspiciously at their motives?"

"You're a beautiful, talented woman, Gretchen," Natalie said. "You may not have felt that way when you were a teenager or just in college, but you're on the verge of being in your thirties. Don't you feel differently about yourself after your successes in life?"

"I did. I thought I was doing better and I was even considering putting up an online dating profile, but I have to tell you there's nothing quite like a movie star to bring out your insecurities."

"May I ask how you've gotten this far in life without losing your virginity?" Amelia looked at her with concern in her eyes. It was the same look guys tended to give her when she told them the truth. Like she was damaged somehow.

Gretchen shrugged. "I didn't date in high school. College was hit-or-miss, but nothing ever got serious enough. As I got older, it got harder. It felt more like a burden, which made it even harder to admit to it. With the few guys I've dated in the last couple of years, they push for sex until they find out I haven't done it before, then they back off. They don't want the responsibility for being my first, or they think I'm going to get clingy because of it… I don't know. It just seems like the longer I wait, the harder it is."

"We can fix this," Bree said brightly. "With your new makeover and your new attitude, we can get you a hot guy, pronto."

"I don't want a—" Gretchen tried to argue, but was drowned out.

"We don't just want to get her laid, Bree," Amelia argued. "We want her to find real happiness in a healthy relationship that includes sexual intimacy."

"I'm not sure I'm—"

"She's waited this long, it should be special."

"Just stop!" Gretchen shouted. The others were working hard at fixing all her problems, but that wasn't what she wanted. "See, this is what I wanted to avoid. I don't need to be fixed up or pimped out. It just is what it is."

"Are you happy with the status quo?" Amelia pressed.

"Some days yes, some days no. But the point of this whole thing is that it makes it harder for me to pretend with Julian. I am awkward enough without being around someone that is completely unattainable in real life."

"I don't know," Bree said thoughtfully. "I think you could have him. You're looking mighty fine today."

"You've lost your mind," Gretchen muttered. If there was one thing she hated, it was being the center of attention. It made her extremely uncomfortable. She was desperate to shift this conversation in another direction. "Now you all know my deep dark secrets, so either help me put out tablecloths or return to your battle stations. There's nothing more to see here."

Bree finished laying out one more tablecloth, then she joined the other two as they slipped out to their offices and kitchen to return to work. Gretchen was relieved to be in the ballroom by herself again.

That was uncomfortable, but it was over, thankfully. She'd never have to confess it to her friends and coworkers again. But she was sure she hadn't heard the end of it. Once this nonsense with Julian wasn't taking up her time, she had no doubt one of them would try to fix her up. They'd tried before, just attempting to help her find a guy, but now it would be a mission.

Laying out the last tablecloth, she looked across the room, which was like a checkerboard stretching out in front of her. In two days, she would be in this room as a guest instead of an employee. It was an odd thought, especially considering she'd be on Julian Cooper's arm.

She couldn't believe Bree actually thought that Julian could be the one to relieve her of the burden of her virginity. That was ridiculous, even with her secret knowledge that he was aroused by kissing her. There was a far leap between those two things. She was paid to be his date in public, not in private. If he actually slept with her, it would be because he wanted her.

There was no way in hell he wanted her. Or did he?

Julian pulled his nondescript black rental SUV into the parking lot at From This Moment. He really didn't need to come here today. Today was a day of relaxation, small errands and final preparation for the big event. At least for the men. The women had gathered for a spa day in the morning, and this afternoon, they were having a bridal tea downtown. That left their male counterparts a day to themselves.

The day had started for them at the golf course. The weather at that hour was a little brisk for Julian's California blood, but the skies were clear and they had a good time playing. They'd all had lunch at some famous hole-in-the-wall barbecue joint, where Julian had a grilled chicken breast and one glorious hush puppy, and then they returned to the hotel and went their separate ways.

With that done, Julian was able to clean up and get ready to do a few chores for the day. There were no messages on his phone from his family, nothing to concern him, so he could focus on wedding preparation. He needed to pick up the tuxedos and get the wedding rings from the jeweler. As the best man, Murray didn't ask much of him. Running a couple errands and throwing a decent bachelor party Friday night were all that was required. It wasn't hard.

And yet he found himself thinking he should pick up Gretchen and bring her along with him.

She wasn't expecting him to show up. He knew she had work to do and his sudden arrival would likely throw her off her game. He told himself he needed to keep her on her toes, because the press certainly would, and she had to be ready for anything.

But in truth, he just wanted to see her again.

It was hard to explain—a feeling he hadn't experienced in a long time. Lately, he'd dated his costars, women he saw on the set every day. He'd gotten used to that sort of immersive dating pattern. So last night, when he'd realized he wouldn't see Gretchen until Friday evening at the rehearsal dinner, he'd felt a little… lonely. He found he missed her awkward smiles and sarcastic comments under her breath. He wanted to wrap his arms around her waist and kiss her until she blushed down into her cleavage.

He didn't realize he was driving to the wedding chapel until he saw the sign ahead of him. By then, he figured it couldn't hurt to pop in and see if she had the time to join him.

Turning off the engine, he climbed out of the SUV and went in the front entrance. The lobby was huge and shaped almost like a cross, with four arched doorways leading to different areas of the chapel. In the center was a round table draped in white with a sheer fabric over it. It looked as if tiny musical notes were stitched all over with shiny black thread, beads and crystals. A tall silver tree branch came up out of the center. Hanging from it were strands of crystal, musical notes and little white cards with people's names on them.

Fancy.

To his left was the wedding chapel, and straight ahead was the reception hall, so he opted to go right, where the offices were. He found a closed door with Gretchen McAlister's name on it and knocked softly.

"No, I don't want to date your cousin!" he heard her shout from the other side of the door.

With a smile, he opened the door, peeking his head in to see her sitting at her desk, tying black and white ribbons around glass cylinders with candles in them. "But you've never even met my cousin. You might like him."

Gretchen's gaze shot up at the sound of his voice, her eyes widening. "Julian! Sorry about that. I thought you were Bree. What are you doing here? Is there a problem? I thought we weren't getting together until tomorrow."

"No problem," he said, slipping into her office and shutting the door behind him. "I just thought you might like to hang out with me today."

Her gaze narrowed at him. "Hang out? Do you mean practice some more? Go over our cover story again?"

Julian shook his head. "No, you've got that covered, I think. I've got to run a couple errands today and I thought you might like to join me, that's all."

Her eyebrows drew together as she considered his offer. She seemed genuinely confused by it. That, or suspicious again. He still didn't understand that. "I'm not dressed up for an official day out with you."

Her hand ran self-consciously over her hair, which was pulled back into a butterfly clip. Her makeup was done, but not heavy-handed. She was wearing a pair of skinny jeans and a simple V-neck sweater with boots. The dark brown of the sweater matched her eyes and made her skin look even creamier against the rich tones. She looked great to him. He actually had a hard time tearing his gaze away from the tantalizing glimpse of cleavage that her sweater teased at, without being too blatant. "You look great," he countered.

"I've also got a lot to do," she said, uncertainty in her voice.

"Well, it just so happens that I don't have a lot to do. How about a little trade-off? You come with me to do a few wedding-related chores, and then I'll come back here with you and help you do whatever it is you do."

A delicate dark eyebrow raised at him. "You're going to help me?"

"Sure," he said with a winning smile. "I have no clue what needs to be done, but I'm an actor. I can fake it."

Gretchen snorted and shook her head. "Well, I'm not sure how much help you'll be, but any help would be great."

Julian chuckled. "Well, thank goodness you have

low standards. Let's go. I have to pick up the tuxedos and the rings."

He helped Gretchen into her coat, and they left the chapel a moment later. As they got into his rental, he admitted, "I also have no idea where I'm going. Do you know where Couture Connection is? That's where I have to get the tuxedos. I can look it up on my phone if we need to."

Gretchen nodded and pointed to the right. "I know where it is. It's just a couple miles from here. Go out to the right."

That part of the day went smoothly enough. They found the store and waited a few minutes to pick up their suits. It wasn't until they were getting ready to leave that Julian noticed the guy across the street with a camera.

He sighed. They'd finally found him. It had actually taken longer than he expected. "Someone tipped off the paparazzi," he said to Gretchen, although he gave a meaningful glance at the girl behind the counter. She'd been in the back room far, far too long in his opinion. She bit her lip and handed over the suits without comment.

"What do we do?" Gretchen asked. "I told you I'm not camera-ready today."

He shrugged. "We do what we need to do. If life stopped just because someone was taking my picture, I'd never get anything done." Julian draped the suits over his arm and reached out to grasp Gretchen's hand. "Off we go," he said.

By the time they reached the jewelry store, there were three cars tailing them, and they were bolder than before. Julian hadn't even opened the car door for

Gretchen before there were four guys swarming the car with cameras, snapping pictures and asking questions.

"Who's the lady, Julian?"

"Her name is Gretchen McAlister," he said, opening the door and helping her out of the car. Normally he would just ignore them, but what was the point of having a fake girlfriend if he wasn't going to publicize that fact?

"Is this your new lady love?" another one prompted, making Gretchen blush.

Julian took her hand and looked into her eyes. It was easy to get lost there, the feelings she evoked in him lately hardly an act. "She's very special to me," he answered with a sincere smile.

"What do you think Bridgette will think of your new relationship?"

"I really don't care what she thinks," Julian said and leaned into Gretchen's ear. "Let's get inside."

The cameras stayed outside while they met with the jeweler. The woman at the counter left them for a moment to go back and find the owner. Julian watched Gretchen peruse the case, her eyes lighting up as she spied something interesting. It was always dangerous to go into a jewelry store with the women he dated. It almost always cost him more than he expected.

"What do you see?" he asked, curious as to what would spark such a reaction in Gretchen. She didn't seem to wear much jewelry.

"That necklace," she said, pointing out a teardrop-shaped opal, speckled with blue and pink fire. "That's my birthstone. I've never seen a natural opal with such bright fire in it before."

It was pretty, and not at all what he expected her to

choose in the case of flashy diamonds and other glittering and expensive gemstones. He doubted Bridgette even knew what an opal was. Julian hovered, waiting for the expectant look he was used to seeing, but Gretchen just shrugged and continued down the case. She continued to surprise him. Perhaps she deserved a surprise in return.

"Mr. Cooper," the owner of the store greeted them as he came out from the back room. "Come with me. I have everything ready for you."

They were taken to a private room in the back where they could inspect the rings and sign for them. There was a lot of gold and a lot of diamonds involved, so he wanted to make sure everything was perfect for Murray and Kelly.

"Is there anything else I can do for you today, Mr. Cooper?" the jeweler asked.

"Actually, yes. That opal teardrop necklace in the case. I'd like that for my companion, please."

The man nodded. "An excellent choice." He called out to the woman at the counter to bring it back to them.

Julian ignored the stunned look on Gretchen's face as the jeweler presented the necklace on a velvet tray. "It looks perfect, thank you."

"Would you like it boxed up?"

"No, we'll be wearing it out." Julian reached for the necklace and unfastened the clasp. Before Gretchen could breathe a word of argument, he rose from his chair to stand behind her. He gently brushed a loose strand of dark hair from her neck, then draped the necklace at her throat. When fastened, the gem fell right beneath her collarbone and was highlighted nicely by the low plunge of her sweater.

"Lovely," the jeweler said. "I'll put the box in the bag with the rings for you."

Julian handed over his black American Express card as the jeweler left the room.

"What is this for?" she finally said when they were alone. "This necklace was super expensive."

He could only shrug and dismiss it the same way she'd dismissed the idea of getting the necklace. "It made you smile," he said. "That was worth every penny."

Gretchen gripped the pendant in her hand, shaking her head. "I'm already being paid a ridiculous amount for this. You don't have to buy me anything."

Julian tried not to flinch at that unfortunate reminder. He'd nearly forgotten that she was being paid to be with him. She was so unlike all the other people in his life with their hands out that it was an unwelcome shock to remember she was getting her piece of him just like the rest. And yet he somehow knew that she was different.

In the end it didn't matter. He wanted to buy the necklace and he bought it. "It's a gift. Enjoy it."

The jeweler returned with his card and receipt. "Anything else I can do for you today?"

As they stood, Julian considered the reporters outside waiting for them. He'd spied a little café up the block, but he didn't want them following the two of them there. He wanted some quiet time with Gretchen before the wedding chaos began.

"Just one more thing. Do you have a rear exit we could use?"

Five

"Is that all you're going to eat?" Gretchen asked. "Seriously, I can't have those camera guys show up and document me here with a full plate while you pick at a spinach salad with no dressing."

"I told you," he said with a smile, "I'm saving up for that cake of Amelia's."

Gretchen looked down at her sandwich and shrugged before taking another bite. "You could at least have the decency to order more food for appearances and just not eat it."

"No one is looking at us, Gretchen. We're hidden in the back corner of a tiny café. Relax and enjoy your food."

Gretchen took a few more bites before she worked up the nerve to ask Julian a question. "Do you ever get tired of it?"

"Tired of what?"

"Tired of being treated like a piece of meat?"

Julian smothered a snort of laughter. "Actually, yes, I do. But I won't look like this forever. I'm young, in my physical prime, so I thought I should make the most of it while I can. I suppose I can tackle some meatier scripts when I'm older and people aren't that interested in my biceps anymore."

"It's not your biceps," Gretchen corrected. "It's the abs."

One of Julian's dark eyebrows went up. "Well, thank you for noticing."

Gretchen blushed. "I didn't. I was really just saying that I…" Her voice drifted off as she ran out of argument.

"It's okay, Gretchen. You're allowed to admire the abs. It would be hypocritical of me to use my body to make money, then criticize someone for noticing it. Maybe someday I'll be known for something else."

"Have you considered doing different kinds of films now? I mean, how many big action flicks can you make in a year? You'd think you'd have time to do something new every now and then."

Julian sighed. "I'd love to. I've actually got a script in my hotel room for something I'm really excited about. It's totally different for me. A real, meaty role. The kind that might earn critical acclaim for my acting."

Gretchen noticed Julian perk up in his seat as he talked about the plot of the script. He was eyeing the role of an alcoholic who loses everything and returns home to face the family he'd left behind. It sounded like an amazing role, the kind that could change the whole trajectory of his career. "Why don't you do it?"

"My manager doesn't think it's a good idea. And

he's right. The more I think about it, the more I know it isn't the right time."

"Why? What could it hurt to try it?"

Julian got a distant look in his eyes as he turned to glance out toward the front of the café. "It could hurt everything. I'm blessed to have what I do now. I have enough money coming in to care for my family, live an amazing life and never worry about how I'm going to pay for something. But this industry is fickle, and you can lose it all in an instant."

"How could you possibly do such a terrible job that you could sink your entire career?"

"It's been a while since I've stretched my serious acting muscles, Gretchen. I may not have even been any good at it to begin with. I landed my first movie role for my body, and little has changed. What if I…" His voice trailed off. "What if I tried to do a serious movie and I'm no good? What if I get panned left, right and center, ripped apart by critics for thinking I could do anything more than shoot a gun or fly a helicopter?"

"At least you will have tried. Pardon me for saying so, but these action movies don't really seem to fulfill you. As a creative person, I understand how that can be. If you're compromising and not doing what you love, eventually you'll lose your joy for the work."

"You enjoy your work, don't you? I can tell by the way your whole demeanor changes when you talk about it."

Gretchen hadn't noticed that before, and she was surprised Julian had paid that much attention. "I'm not sure about how it changes me, but I do love my job. I'm not necessarily a traditional artist that paints or sculpts, but I get to do so many different and creative things. I never get bored. And I get to work with my best friends, so that makes every day fun."

"I have to admit I'm jealous."

Gretchen looked up at him, her eyes wide in surprise. "You're jealous of me? Really?"

He nodded. "Absolutely. You're living the life you want. You're doing the job you enjoy. You seem to be living so authentically, doing what makes you happy."

"Well, I'm also not a millionaire. There's probably a trade-off in there somewhere."

"Money isn't all it's cracked up to be. It's necessary, and I'm thankful to have enough to do what I need to do, but the thought of losing it can become what holds you back. I mean, look at me. I'm in a delightful-smelling café, near drooling over some berry tart in the case that I won't let myself have. I don't eat what I want, I don't do what I want, I don't act in the films I'd like to…all because of the money."

Gretchen shook her head. "Only someone with money could ever consider it a burden."

Julian watched her curiously for a moment. "May I ask why you agreed to participate in this charade with me?"

She had to laugh at his query. She was surprised it had taken him this long to ask. "That's a good question. For the first few days, I was asking myself the same thing. Part of it was being in the right place at the wrong time, but in the end, I'm ashamed to admit it came down to the money. It was a few days out of my life and when it was over, I'd have the opportunity to take the trip I've always dreamed of taking. Without it, who knows when, if ever, I'd get another chance."

"I love to travel," Julian said, scooting aside his half-eaten salad and leaning closer to her. "Where are you wanting to go?"

"Italy," she said with a wistful sigh. "It's been my dream since high school when we studied the Renaissance. I want to go and just suck up all the beauty there. The paintings, the architecture, the food and the people. I want to experience it all, and this money will make that possible."

Julian nodded as he listened to her speak. "Italy is beautiful. You'll love it."

"Have you been?"

"Once. We filmed for a few weeks in Tuscany and I got to visit Florence. It's an amazing place. I've always wanted to go back, but I haven't had the time."

Gretchen understood that. "I know how you feel. Even with the money, taking the time away from From This Moment is hard to do. It's been my life since we started the place."

"Well," he said, "I think you need to make the time. If you've got the money, do it. There's never going to be a perfect time, and before you know it, life will dwindle away your savings and you'll miss your chance."

"I don't think I—"

"I dare you to go next spring," Julian said with a conspiratorial smile. "Maybe late April or early May. It will be perfect. Good weather and not too crowded yet."

Gretchen nearly choked. "You *dare* me?"

"I do," he said, his blue eyes focused intently on her in a way that made her spine soften and her chest tighten. "You don't seem like the kind of woman that would back down from a dare."

She eyed him with a twist of her lips. She hadn't played many games of truth or dare in her time, but she was certain that two could play at this game. "Very well, I accept. But I have a dare for you as well."

"Oh, you do now?" He sat back in his seat and crossed his arms over his chest as though he couldn't be intimidated by her challenge. "I can't wait to hear what it is. Back in college, I always opted for the dare over the truth. I haven't turned one down, ever."

That might be true, but he hadn't gone up against Gretchen before. "Okay, Mr. Confident. I dare you to go back to the counter, buy that berry tart you want so badly and eat every bite of it. Live on the wild side for just today, Julian. Who knows, one day it's berry tarts, the next day it's a film premiering at Sundance."

Julian watched her face for a moment. She knew that he was fighting with himself, but a dare was a dare, right?

She decided maybe she should throw him a bone. She of all people knew what it was like to try to diet and have family and friends unintentionally sabotage her plans. "I'll share it with you, if you want."

At that, his expression brightened. "Done." He got up and left her alone at the table for a few minutes to secure their pastry prize.

Alone, she sat back in her chair and took the first deep breath for nearly half an hour. Julian was so intense, she sometimes found it hard to breathe when he was around. But she liked it. She liked being with him. She'd never expected that to be the case. They were so different, or so she thought.

Beneath it all, she realized they had more in common than she expected. The more time they spent together, the more easily she was able to see the man behind the actor.

As nice as that was, they were dangerous, pointless thoughts. They'd just discussed what she was going to do with the money he was paying her to be around him. Once the wedding was over, so was their time together. It might feel as if they had a connection, but he was an actor. Gretchen couldn't let herself forget that. In a few days, he would return to LA and forget she ever existed.

It was just her luck that the first guy she'd really felt comfortable with in years turned out to be a Hollywood actor who would disappear and want nothing more to do with her.

At this rate, she was never going to get laid.

Julian nearly groaned as he took the last bite of the berry tart. It was the best thing he'd tasted in…a year, maybe? Most days of his life, he didn't control what he ate. His trainers and personal chefs took care of that for him and kept the temptations far away. Bridgette was even more strict with her eating, so it was easier to get through the day knowing he wouldn't be exposed to the things he really wanted. Out of sight, out of mind.

Gretchen wasn't hung up on all that. She indulged when she wanted to indulge, and the satisfied smile on her face was evidence of that. So what if it cost her a few extra pounds? Her soft, womanly figure with a sincere smile was far better than rail-thin Bridgette and her pinched, anxious look. She never smiled with contentment. She was always looking for something more in life.

This berry tart may have been that very thing.

"So naughty," Gretchen said, putting her fork down on the empty plate. "I bet you gain three whole pounds eating that."

Julian sat up sharply. "That's not possible. Is it?"

She laughed at him and shook her head. "No. You're fine. Half a berry tart isn't the end of the world. You did get a serving of fiber-rich fruit out of it, after all."

That's when Julian noticed a small dab of strawberry glaze at the corner of her lips. He reached for his napkin to dab it away, but hesitated. He had a better idea.

"Hold still," he said, leaning across the table toward her. With one hand gently caressing her neck, he pressed his lips to the corner of her mouth, removing the last of their dessert before moving over and kissing her.

Just like every time he touched her, Julian immediately responded to Gretchen. With her soft lips pressed against his and the scent of her skin filling his lungs, he couldn't pull away. Every muscle in his body tightened with a building need for her. Each time they kissed, his desire for her grew. He knew that this was a business arrangement, but he couldn't help his reaction to her. He wanted her more than he'd wanted any other woman before.

But unlike the other times when they were practicing making it look good for the cameras, this time Gretchen pulled away from him.

He wasn't expecting it, and her sudden withdrawal left him hovering, vulnerable, over the table. "What's the matter?"

She watched him with wary dark eyes. "What was that about?"

His brows went up. "What was the kiss about?"

"Yes." She glanced around the café, her gaze dropping into her lap. "I thought you said we were done practicing that. There's no one watching us right now."

Gretchen couldn't fathom that he would kiss her just

because he could. Because he *wanted* to. "That kiss," he said, "wasn't for the cameras. That one was for me."

Her eyes met his with a narrowed gaze and a frown wrinkling her nose. "I don't understand."

Julian reached across the table and took her hand. "What is there to understand, Gretchen? I like you. I wanted to kiss you, so I did. That's pretty simple boy-meets-girl kind of stuff."

She nodded, although he wasn't entirely sure she felt better about the whole thing. "I told you before I'm not that good with the boy-meets-girl thing."

She had told him, but he didn't realize until that moment how serious she was about it. How was it possible that she couldn't understand why he'd want to kiss her? Was her self-esteem so low that she didn't think she was worthy of his attention? If so, he'd see to correcting that assumption right away.

"You said you like me. What did you mean by that?"

"I mean that I like you. And yes, that I'm attracted to you. I know this arrangement is mostly about business, and I don't want to make you feel uncomfortable, but I'm into you, Gretchen. Truly."

She responded with silence, reaching out to take a sip of her iced tea. It was almost as though she didn't know how to respond, as if he'd said "I love you" too soon in a relationship. Had he read the signals wrong? He didn't want her to think that he presumed their contract extended to extracurricular activities in the bedroom. He was about to say something to soften the statement when she looked up at him with an intensity in her chocolate-brown eyes.

"I'm attracted to you, as well," she said boldly.

Julian shelved the instinctual smile. He didn't want

her to think he was laughing at her. It was anything but. He had suspected that she was turned on by him, but he couldn't know for sure. Knowing made him feel lighter somehow. "I'm glad we got that out there."

She nodded, and her gaze returned to her lap. Any fantasies he had about taking her back to his hotel room and making love to her that instant fizzled away. One step at a time, he reminded himself. Besides, they had work they were avoiding. Even if she wanted him as desperately as he wanted her, there was a wedding coming up, and the ballroom needed to be decorated sooner rather than later.

"I guess we'd better get back to the chapel," he said. "I promised I'd help you set up all those decorations, remember?"

"You don't really have to," she said dismissively. "You bought my food, and more importantly, this necklace. I'll happily stay up all night decorating on my own to make up for the lost time."

He shook his head. "You're not getting rid of me so easily. I may not have an artistic eye, but I'm helping you and that's final."

Gretchen nodded and placed her napkin on the table. "It's been over an hour. Do you think the photographers have given up or are they still sitting outside the jewelry store?"

Julian shrugged and got up from the table. "It doesn't matter. I'm happy we had the hour alone that we had." He took her hand and led her out of the café. The cameramen had given up, and their vehicle was waiting patiently for them down the block.

The return to the chapel was uneventful, yet awkwardly silent. Not since their first night together had there been this weird energy between them. It continued until they were back in the ballroom and the work began. They lost themselves in tying a black organza bow around the back of each chair. Julian was quickly removed from that task—apparently he didn't tie bows, just knots—and he was given the job of folding all the linen napkins. Thank goodness there wasn't some fancy fabric origami going on, just a simple fold that created a rectangle with a pocket.

When the bows were finished, Gretchen laid a glass charger with silver beaded accents at each place setting. Julian followed behind her, draping the napkin across the charger and slipping the menu into the pocket. He helped her carry in about forty of the decorated hurricane vases, placing them on the stage along with some large silver vases and candelabras.

"What next?" he asked. "Do these need to go on the tables?"

Gretchen sat down on the edge of the stage and shook her head. "Not tonight." She glanced at her cell phone. "It's getting late. I'll do that tomorrow."

Julian sat beside her and eyed the room. They had gotten a lot done, but if he knew Gretchen, there was a lot more in store for the decor. "Are you sure? I can stay as late as you need me to."

"Aren't you here for Murray? Shouldn't you guys be hanging out and playing poker or something? Guy bonding?"

He shrugged. "Not really. We golfed and ate barbecue today before I came over. Tomorrow, there's just the rehearsal, the dinner and the bachelor party."

Gretchen gave him a knowing smile. "Whatcha got planned? Strippers and beer?"

"No," he said with an offended tone to his voice. "It's going to be classy! I've rented out an old piano bar downtown. I've also got a Cuban guy coming in to roll authentic cigars and a local microbrewery doing flights of all their best beers. A few ladies from the burlesque show will be performing." He tried to say it all with a straight face, but it didn't last long. She had him pegged the first time. "Okay, yeah," he laughed. "Strippers and beer. But they're expensive strippers and beer."

"I'm sure that makes it a much classier affair," she said with a smile.

"I thought so."

"We'd better get you home, then. You'll need your rest for a long night of debauchery." Gretchen stood up and dusted her hands off on her jeans.

Julian followed her out of the ballroom, waiting as she switched off lights and locked doors behind her. When they stepped outside into the parking lot, he noticed the temperature had really dropped since they went inside. In just a few short hours, it had gone from a California November day to a November day anywhere else. He snuggled into his leather jacket, but all it really did was keep the wind from cutting through him.

Gretchen seemed more prepared. She stepped outside in a dark burgundy peacoat and a scarf. He walked her over to her tiny sedan, hesitant to say good-night and hesitant to say what he needed to say to make the night last. He moved close to tell her goodbye, her back pressed to the car as she looked up at him with the overhead lights twinkling in her eyes.

"Do you have a real coat?" she asked when she noticed him start to shiver.

"Not with me. I have one I wear when I go skiing

in Aspen, but I didn't think I'd need it here." Looking at the space between them, he realized he could see his breath. It was darn cold. He should've looked more closely at the forecast before he packed.

"Well, maybe tomorrow you should take a trip to the store and pick up a nice wool coat. We can't let the best man catch cold the day before the wedding."

"That's a good idea. Perhaps you can just help me stay warm in the meantime."

With a smile, Gretchen wrapped her arms around his neck and pulled him close. Her lips mere centimeters from his, she asked, "How's this?"

Julian pressed the full length of his body against her and wrapped his arms around her waist. "Definitely getting warmer. Still a little cold, though."

Holding his face in her hands, she guided his lips to hers. A surge of heat shot through his veins as they touched. When her tongue grazed along his own, he was nearly warm enough to take off his jacket. That simple, innocent touch was enough to set his blood to boiling with need for her.

He traveled the line of her jaw, leaving a trail of kisses until he reached the sensitive curve of her neck. Gretchen gasped and clung to him as he nibbled at her flesh. The sound was like music to his ears, sending a chill through his whole body. Desperate to touch more of her, he moved one hand from her waist, sliding it up her side until it cupped her breast.

He was rewarded with another gasp, but it was quickly followed by insistent palms pressing against his chest. He moved back, dropping his hands to his sides. "What's the matter?" he asked between panting breaths.

"I…" she started, then shook her head. "It's just a little too fast for me, Julian."

Fast? "It's Thursday, Gretchen. By Monday, I'll be back in California. I don't want to make you uncomfortable, but we don't have forever."

Gretchen sighed and shifted her gaze to look over his shoulder. "I know."

"What's really bothering you?" It didn't seem as though her body and her words were lining up. "Tell me."

Swallowing hard, she nodded. "I told you I hadn't dated much, but it's more than that, Julian. It's not that I don't want you. I do. Very badly. And I would gladly take this as far as you're willing to go. But I think if you knew the truth, you'd…"

"I'd what?" He couldn't think of anything she could say to smother his desire for her.

"I'm a virgin," she said, almost spitting out the words as if to get them out before she could change her mind.

Julian's eyes widened and he stumbled back, as though her words had physically hit him. Was she serious? "A virgin?" he asked.

"Yes. Like I said, it isn't a problem for me. Frankly, you'd be doing me a huge favor by ridding me of this burden I've carried around for all these years. But I find that people don't react well to the news."

He could understand that. He wasn't reacting that well himself. It wasn't as though she'd just announced she was a hermaphrodite or something, but still, it had caught him off guard. In an instant, the idea of a fun, casual romance while he was in Nashville had just gotten instantly more complicated.

"Damn," Gretchen whispered.

Her curse snapped him out of his own head. He looked at her with a frown. "What?"

"It's happened again," she said. "I've scared you off. You can't get away from me fast enough. I can see it in your eyes."

"No, no," he said, shaking his head adamantly. "It's just not what I was expecting. But I should've…" His voice trailed away. All the signs had pointed there; he just hadn't thought it was possible.

"Well, it's getting late and you're probably freezing," he said, the words sounding lame even to his own ears. "We've got a long night tomorrow, so I'll let you get home. I'll see you here at the rehearsal at six?"

"Yeah." Gretchen didn't even try to hide the disappointment on her face and in her voice. His quick backpedaling had hurt her feelings, but he didn't know what else to do. "Good night, Julian."

Without so much as a goodbye peck on the cheek, she opened her car door and got inside. He'd barely closed the door when the engine roared to life and she backed out of the parking space.

As her taillights disappeared into the distance, Julian realized he was a schmuck. Apparently he was much better with women when he had a script to follow.

Six

Gretchen should've kept her damn mouth shut. That was it—she wasn't telling a guy the truth again. The next time she got someone interested in sleeping with her, she'd let him find out the hard way. It might be rough going, but by the time he realized it, it would be done and she wouldn't have to go through this embarrassment again and again.

At the moment, it would be easy to believe that nothing had happened last night. She and Julian were seated together at a table with a few other members of the wedding party. The rehearsal dinner was wrapping up, and waiters were coming around with trays of desserts. His arm was draped over her shoulder, a devoted smile on his face whenever he looked at her. Ever the actor, this was easy for him. It wasn't so easy for her, especially with Bree hovering around the edge of the room taking pictures and smiling knowingly at her.

Just when she thought she'd overcome all the potential problems with this fake dating scenario, she'd screwed it up. She should've just kept it fake. By admitting in the coffee shop that she was attracted to him, it had opened up the charade to more. He liked her, she liked him…what was stopping this public relationship from becoming a private one?

A hymen, that's what.

The look on Julian's face when she said the words had been heartbreaking. One minute, he'd looked at her with blue eyes hooded with desire. She had no doubt in that moment that he sincerely wanted her. Not even her fragile ego could believe otherwise. Then, in a flash, it was replaced by panic. She knew the moment the words left her mouth that it was a mistake.

Julian wanted fun, flirty sex. A hot wedding hookup. Deflowering some thirty-year-old virgin probably didn't line up with his plans. She'd accused him of trying to escape, but at that point, she wanted out of there more desperately than he did. She needed plenty of time to get home, lie in bed and kick herself.

Fortunately, today had been about wedding preparations. She spent most of the afternoon getting things in place in the chapel before the rehearsal. That kept her busy enough that she could keep her embarrassing incident far out of her mind. When she did see Julian again, there wasn't much time to talk. First was the rehearsal, and he was on the platform with Murray and Kelly. After that, they all got ushered onto a limo bus and taken to the restaurant for the rehearsal dinner. They hadn't had two seconds alone, much less time to talk.

Part of her was okay with that. She didn't feel the need to analyze last night with him. She just needed to get through the next two days and put all of this behind her. But it was hard when he was always touching her. Holding her hand, hugging her to his side, whispering in her ear. It just made her want what she was destined not to have that much more intensely.

One of the waiters placed a piping hot ramekin of peach cobbler in front of her with vanilla bean ice cream melting over it. It looked amazing, and the thought of a tasty treat was enough to rouse her from her dark thoughts. She needed to play the happy girlfriend regardless of what was going on between them.

"That looks good," Julian said, leaning in to examine her dessert. "Decadent, actually."

"Didn't you get dessert?" she asked, already knowing the answer but trying to make polite conversation.

He shook his head and took a sip of his water. He'd spent the evening nibbling on blackened tilapia and roasted vegetables. "Just because you dared me to eat that berry tart doesn't mean I've thrown my clean eating lifestyle out the window."

"Would you like just one bite? I mean, I know you don't want to be first, but I thought you might want the second bite." She couldn't help getting that dig in under the veiled discussion of dessert so the others at the table couldn't follow the twists and turns of their relationship.

A look of surprise lit up Julian's face, his lips twisting into an amused smile. "For the record, I don't mind having the first taste. I just feel guilty getting the first bite when I know I can't stay around to eat the whole thing."

"The cobbler won't be offended, I assure you. It just wants to be eaten while it's still hot and juicy. Before long, it's going to be a cold, crusty, bitter mess."

"I sincerely doubt that. I know turning that treat down last night was a mistake, but as it was, I spent two hours in the hotel gym last night."

Her gaze met his. "Feeling guilty?"

He nodded. "I had a little pent-up energy after I left you. Ten miles on the treadmill helped, but I still felt like crap when I was done."

"You can run all you want, but if you're on a treadmill, you aren't getting any farther from your problems."

"Wise words," he agreed. "Exercise does help me think. If nothing else, I got some...clarity."

Gretchen narrowed her gaze at him, her heart suddenly leaping to life in her chest. "What does that mean?"

"It means we need to talk."

She rolled her eyes and turned back to her dessert. Talk? She'd done plenty of that already. If all he wanted to do was talk, she was going to save this poor cobbler from her own fate. She picked up her spoon and scooped up a bite, stopping as Julian leaned in.

"Soon," he whispered into her ear. The spoon trembled in her hand as she held it in midair. "I don't know when, but soon. Don't you worry about that dessert going uneaten."

Gretchen drew in a ragged breath. Suddenly, she wasn't that hungry for cobbler anymore. The idea that she might be naked in front of him in the near future was an appetite killer.

"So, Julian," one of the bridesmaids called across the table. "Are you guys ready for the bachelor party tonight?"

Julian sat up and flashed his charming smile at the

others seated with them. "Absolutely. I've got a great night planned for the boys."

One of the other women looked at her date with a warning glance. "Try to limit yourself to one lap dance, please."

The man laughed. "Why? I'm not the one getting married tomorrow. You afraid I'll be tempted by the goods?"

The brunette shook her head. "No, I'm worried you'll stick your whole paycheck in her panties and come back to me broke."

"Well, if I do, maybe Julian can help me out. I heard you made fifteen million for your last movie. Is that true?"

Gretchen felt Julian stiffen beside her. For the first time while they were together, he was the nervous one. He'd mentioned a few times about how people seemed to come to him with their hands out. This guy didn't even know Julian, not really. It was veiled as a joke, but it wasn't funny. She didn't like seeing Julian react that way.

"And exactly how much money did *you* make last year?" she piped up before Julian could respond.

The man's eyes grew wide at her sharp tone and he immediately held up his hands in surrender. "Sorry," he said. "It was a joke. I mean, if I made that much money, I'd be shouting it from the rooftops."

"And everyone, including the IRS and some guy you don't even know at a rehearsal dinner, would be knocking on your front door looking for their piece."

The large, burly groomsman seemed to disappear into himself. "I'm going to go get a drink from the bar," he said, getting up and crossing the room. The other people turned to each other and started talking among themselves to avoid the awkward turn in the conversation.

"Rawr." Julian leaned in and growled into her ear. "I didn't know you were such a tiger."

Gretchen chuckled. "Neither did I. But I couldn't sit there and say nothing. Just because you're a public figure doesn't mean it's any of his business how much you make."

Julian smiled. "It isn't as exciting as it sounds anyway. I mean, I have plenty, don't get me wrong, but the bigger the life, the bigger the expenses. The mortgage on my house in Beverly Hills is nearly thirty thousand a month."

Gretchen nearly choked on her sip of wine. "That's insane."

"That's California real estate for you. Add in the ridiculous property taxes and insurance, security, staff… it adds up. Uncle Sam gets his whopping cut, then Ross, then my accountant."

"Do I need to give this necklace back?"

"No, of course not. I wouldn't live in a five-million-dollar house if I couldn't afford to. Life is just on a different scale when you live this way, is all."

Gretchen shook her head and reached into her purse to find her phone. It was getting late. As much as she was enjoying the dinner and curious to finish her interrupted conversation with Julian, she needed to get back and finish up the ballroom for tomorrow. "I'd better go."

Julian pouted, the frown pulling at the corners of his full mouth. Gretchen wanted to kiss it away, but resisted. Instead, she leaned in and pressed a kiss to his cheek. "You have fun with the boys tonight. Don't let Murray get too hungover. Natalie hates it when the wedding party is teetering on their feet all day."

"Yes, ma'am. I'll walk you out."

"No, no," she insisted, pushing him back into his seat. "I can make it just fine. Your loyalty is to Murray tonight."

Gretchen stood up, and he scooped her hand into his own. He brought it up to his lips, placing a searing kiss on the back of her hand. The heated tingle radiated up her whole arm, making her flush pink against the deep shades of purple fabric that made up her dress.

"I'll see you *soon*," he said, emphasizing the last word. That was the same word he'd used earlier when they spoke about their physical relationship.

She pulled her hand away and tried to cover her reaction with a smile. "Okay," she said. "Good night."

Gretchen gave a parting wave to Murray and Kelly before slipping out. It wasn't until she stepped out that she realized they'd all come in the limo van, including Bree. With a shake of her head, she called a cab and waited patiently outside for it to arrive.

It was just as well. She needed the cold air to cool the fire Julian had so easily built inside her.

Julian was over the bachelor party scene. He'd done his duty and set up a great send-off for Murray, complete with alcohol, scantily clad women and billiards, but it wasn't really where he wanted to spend his time. Not since his discussion with Gretchen at the rehearsal dinner.

He'd relived that moment by her car over and over in his head since it happened. He had expected a lot of different reasons for why she shied away from him, but none of them included the fact that she'd never been with a man before. In this day and age, that sort of thing was almost unheard of.

Admittedly, he hadn't reacted well to the news, and he felt horrible about it. He'd told her about his two-hour treadmill penance, but that wasn't the half of it. He'd barely slept that night thinking about how badly he handled her confession. It hadn't been because he felt as if there were something wrong with her, or that she was strange, but because he'd felt this sudden pressure he wasn't expecting.

Being a woman's first lover was a big responsibility. When he was sixteen and horny, he hadn't thought about it that way, and he knew of at least one girl who'd had a less-than-stellar first time because of how he'd handled it. Now he was a grown man. An experienced lover. It was bad enough that he had a reputation because of his films that he was some hard-bodied Casanova. Adding the delicate handling of a woman's first time on top of that made his chest tighten.

Gretchen had made it sound as though she would be happy to be rid of the burden of her virginity. It would be doing her a favor, somehow. And he wanted her. There was no doubt of that. But was making love to Gretchen selfish? Was taking her virginity and then returning to LA a horrible thing to do, even if she'd asked him to? Just the thought of it made him feel sleazy.

Speaking of sleazy, a woman in a corset and a thong was making her way over to him. She had multiple bills tucked into her G-string and a coat of glitter across her tan skin, reminding him of his own ill-fated turn as a stripper in a movie. The kind of movies he hated.

The kind of films Gretchen encouraged him to branch out from.

The burlesque dancer wrapped her feather boa around Julian's neck to pull him closer. Putting a few obligatory dollars beneath the strap at her hip, he waved her back toward the groom. Murray was the one who deserved the attention tonight, not him.

Julian looked down at his phone to check his messages. He didn't want anything to be wrong at home, but it would give him an excuse to leave. Murray had been his roommate in college, so he knew all about Julian's family and how things tended to crop up. Thankfully, all was well, but unfortunately it was only a little after ten. Was that too soon to leave? He sighed and put his phone away. Probably. The cigar roller hadn't even finished making all the cigars yet.

Then he caught Murray's gaze across the room. His friend smiled and shook his head. "Go," he mouthed silently, then turned back to the busty blonde vying for his attention.

That was all it took. He stood and walked toward the edge of the room, trying to slowly slip out without making a big deal of it. Once he made it out the door, he climbed into his SUV, thankful that they hadn't taken the limo bus directly from the rehearsal dinner so he had a vehicle to make his escape. Inside his car, he texted Gretchen.

Where are you?

As the engine warmed up, he got a response. In the ballroom hanging seventy thousand crystal pendants. Care to join me?

He did. Putting the phone aside, he pulled out of the parking lot and headed back to From This Moment. Once again, Gretchen's little green sedan was the only car in the lot when he arrived. Apparently everyone else had already given up for the night.

He headed straight for the ballroom, as she'd said she'd be there, but he didn't see her. Her handiwork was evident, though. The room had been absolutely transformed since he'd been there the day before. The tables now had an assortment of glasses and flatware at each place setting. The tall silver candelabras he'd moved the night before stood in the center of some tables. Others had slim silver vases or small silver bowls. There were candles scattered all over and tall white trees in the corners, dripping with crystals. It looked as though the only thing missing was the fresh flowers.

"Just wait until the pin lights are on and all the candles are lit," Gretchen said, coming in behind him with a box in her arms. "It will be magical."

"I bet. You're very talented."

Gretchen snorted and moved past him to set the box on the edge of the stage where the band would set up in the morning. She was still wearing the flirty purple dress she'd worn to the rehearsal dinner, only now she was barefoot, having cast aside her heels for the sake of comfort. "You're very kind, but it's a table setting, not a Picasso."

Julian followed her path, slowly coming up behind her as she unpacked tiny attendee gifts to place on the tables. When she stood, he snaked his arms around her waist and pulled her back tight against him. The soft curve of her backside pressed into his desire, suppressing all the reasons why he couldn't be with Gretchen.

What if he could give her something without taking anything away? It might take every ounce of restraint he had, but he wanted this so badly. "I've thought a lot about our discussion at dinner."

Gretchen gasped softly, although he wasn't certain if it was his words or his obvious need for her. "And?" she asked in almost a hushed whisper.

"And it made me wonder." Julian nestled into her neck, planting warm kisses under her earlobe between phrases. "You said you're a virgin, but have you ever had an orgasm before?"

Gretchen chuckled. "Yes, I have. I might be a virgin, but I'm also a grown woman perfectly capable of managing my needs when necessary."

Now Julian had to laugh. She always surprised him, especially with her bold honesty, even in the face of potentially embarrassing questions. "Has someone else ever given you one?" he pressed.

"No."

"I'd like to."

She shivered as he pressed another kiss along the soft skin of her neck. "Um…right now?"

Not the ideal location, but why the hell not? "Yes, right now." His palm slid across her torso, venturing to her low belly, then to the side of her hip and down. He moved until he reached her smooth bare thigh, shifting the hem of her dress a few inches higher to stroke it. Then he stopped. "Unless you'd rather wait," he said.

After a slight hesitation, Gretchen arched her back, pressing the curve of her rear firmly against his erection. "I think twenty-nine years is long enough to wait, don't you?"

"I do."

Julian turned her in his arms so she was facing him. Despite her bold declaration, he could still sense anxiety in her. She bit at her bottom lip, her dark eyes both challenging him and nervously flickering toward the door and back. He could imagine that the mix of emotions was confusing, but he wouldn't let her psych herself out about this. It was happening.

Dipping his head down, he kissed her. She started to relax with the familiar activity, wrapping her arms around his neck. She let her tongue slide boldly along his own, eliciting a low groan deep in his throat. Keeping this all about her pleasure would be hard when she touched him like this, but he could do it. He was determined.

Julian encircled her waist, pulling her toward him and guiding her backward toward the stage. Once her calves met with the wooden platform, he eased her back until she was sitting on the edge. He tore his lips away from hers, lowering himself to his knees in front of her. Gretchen's eyes grew wide as she watched him put his palms on each bare knee.

With his eyes trained on hers, he pressed gently, parting her legs little by little until he could move between them. He slid his hands up her thighs, pushing the purple fabric of her dress up and out of his way, stopping just short of exposing her. He could feel her muscles tense beneath his touch, so he changed his tactic. Julian wanted her fully relaxed for this.

He kissed her again, distracting her with his lips and tongue as he slipped the straps of her dress off her shoulders. It didn't take much for the fabric to slide down, exposing the bra beneath it. He cupped one breast, slowly stroking and teasing at the nipple through the sheer black fabric. Gretchen groaned against his mouth, her reaction encouraging him to break away from the kiss and draw her nipple into his mouth.

Gretchen's head went back, a cry of pleasure escaping her lips. It echoed in the large ballroom like music to his ears. He continued to tease her through the moist fabric, the distraction it provided allowing him to move his hand beneath her skirt. He found that the panties were made of the same sheer material. When his fingers brushed across her most sensitive spot, Gretchen gasped, her hips rising up off the stage.

Julian eased Gretchen back until she was lying on the stage. She protested at first, but he didn't want her nervously watching everything he did. "Just lie back, close your eyes and enjoy it," he said soothingly until the tension eased from her body.

He started by removing her panties. He slid them down her legs, tossing them out of his way. Then he crouched down and started a trail of kisses that ran from the inside of her ankles, up her calves, to her inner thighs. He let his hot breath tease at her center. She squirmed beneath him, the anticipation of it likely building inside her.

Without warning, he let his tongue flick across her flesh. Gretchen cried out, her fingers grasping fruitlessly at the stage beside her. Julian gave her a moment to recover before he did it again. He pressed her thighs farther apart, exposing more of her to him. His fingers and tongue started moving over her in earnest now, the relentless pursuit of her release foremost in his mind.

Gretchen's gasps and groans were an encouraging melody. As they escalated in pitch and intensity, he knew she was getting close. Her thighs were tense beside him, as though they were made of steel. He re-doubled his efforts until a desperate "yes, yes!" filled the room.

Gently, he slipped one finger inside her, knowing it would put her over the edge. He felt her muscles clamp down on him and half a second later, she came undone. She gasped and cried, writhing on the hard stage even as he continued to work over her with his tongue.

It wasn't until she collapsed back against the stage, her thighs trembling, that he pulled away. Her ragged breath was the only sound in the massive ballroom as he smoothed out her skirt and sat back on his heels.

Several minutes later, Gretchen pushed herself up to look at him. Her pale cheeks were flushed red, her eyes glassy, but she was smiling. It made his chest ache to see it. The women in his life always seemed to de-mand so much from him. Gretchen appreciated even the tiniest of gestures.

"Well," she said at last. "I'm never going to look at this ballroom the same way, ever again."

Seven

"Take me to the hotel, Julian."

Julian's gaze met hers, a heat in them she couldn't ignore. And yet he hesitated, swallowing hard before he spoke. "Are you sure?"

"I am." She'd never been so certain of anything in her whole life. She wasn't foolish enough to think this relationship would last past the weekend, or that she would be anything more than a faint memory in Julian's mind, but she couldn't pass this chance up. Even if she *had* been with a man before, making love to a movie star was every woman's sexual fantasy.

And yet the doubts plagued her. Of course she wanted him. But his wanting her was another matter. "Unless you don't want to," she added in a quiet voice.

Julian rolled his eyes and took her hand, tugging her up off the stage. "I want to. You have no idea how much I want to. I just don't know that I should. I can't promise you anything."

Gretchen gazed up at him and shook her head. "All I want you to promise me is a night of hot sex and enough orgasms to last me until the next guy comes along."

Julian smiled, making her relax into his arms. He wasn't turning her down, thank goodness.

"That," he said with a wicked glint in his blue eyes, "I can do."

They left the chapel so quickly, Gretchen barely had time to grab her heels and switch off the lights. The drive to his hotel seemed to take an eternity. In the dark of the car, Gretchen bit at her lower lip and tried to stay in the moment. While her body was still pulsating from the orgasm he'd given her it was easy to propose they go further, but the reality was creeping in with every mile they came nearer to his hotel. She was about to have sex. The idea of it both thrilled and terrified her.

As they walked the length of the hotel corridor together, hand in hand, she could feel her heart pounding in her chest. On the other side of the door was what she'd been fantasizing about since she was sixteen years old.

"Would you like a glass of wine?" he asked as they stepped into his suite.

"No," she shook her head. "I'd rather just…get to it."

Julian frowned at her and crossed his arms over his chest. "Gretchen, this isn't a sprint, it's a marathon."

"I know," she replied, knowing it had come out wrong and right at the same time. She wanted it done so she could put the anxiety aside and enjoy herself.

Julian dropped his arms at his side and approached her, stopping just short of them touching. He placed his large, warm palms on her bare upper arms, rubbing them in a soothing rhythm. "Relax. Enjoy yourself. Unless you change your mind or the hotel catches fire, I guarantee it's going to happen."

Gretchen let out the ragged breath she didn't realize she'd been holding in. As the air rushed from her lungs, so did the tension that had built up in every muscle. "You're right, I'm sorry. I'm just so—"

Julian's lips met hers in an instant, stealing the words from her mouth. His touch made all her worries disappear. She melted into his arms, pressing into the hard body she couldn't get out of her head. Even when she heard the sound of her zipper gliding down her back, she didn't tense up. The glide of his tongue and the hungry press of his fingertips into her flesh made her whole body soften like butter.

He tugged the straps of her dress and bra down her shoulders, planting a line of kisses along her throat and across the newly exposed skin. Julian's hungry gaze flickered over her breasts before he dipped his head to taste the flesh that threatened to spill over the top of her bra.

With her dress open in the back, she could feel the fabric slipping down, pooling at her waist, but she fought the urge to stop it. By all indications, Julian liked what he saw. Tonight it was all coming off, no matter how anxious she might be about it.

Reaching behind her, Julian unfastened the clasp of her bra, sliding it down her arms and draping it across the nearby chair. Her nakedness was immediately covered by his hands and his mouth. Gretchen's eyes fluttered closed as he drew one hard pink nipple into his mouth. A bolt of pleasure shot right through her, mak-

ing her core tighten and ache and her legs start to tremble beneath her.

She was so lost in the moment that when Julian
crouched down and lifted her up into the air, she was
caught completely off guard. With a cry of surprise, she
wrapped her arms around his neck and her legs around
his waist. "You're going to throw your back out or something," she complained as she clung to him. She wasn't
some skinny-minnie supermodel, as though he could
forget with her half naked in his arms.

He narrowed his gaze at her, a challenge in his eyes.
"Gretchen, even on a bad day I can bench press twice
what you weigh. Stop worrying and let me carry you
into the bedroom to ravish you properly, all right?"

Squeezing her eyes shut, she buried her face in his
neck. She couldn't let her stupid insecurities ruin this
moment. With one arm wrapped around her waist, Julian's other slid along her outer thigh, gripping one
round cheek beneath her cocktail dress. She felt his
palm explore her skin in a curious fashion before he
spoke.

"Naughty," he whispered as they started toward the
bedroom.

"What?" She didn't know what he was talking about.

"You never put your panties back on."

Gretchen straightened up in his arms, her eyes wide
as she gasped. "Oh, my God. I left them on the floor
of the ballroom."

Julian chuckled and shook his head, continuing into
the bedroom. "Someone's going to get a surprise first
thing in the morning."

Thoughts of Bree or Natalie running across those
sheer black panties in the ballroom suddenly consumed

her. How embarrassing. Then Julian lowered her onto the bed and her bare back met with the soft, plush fabric of the comforter.

She watched as he unbuttoned his dress shirt and slipped it off, exposing the famously familiar muscles beneath it. God, he was beautiful. There was a Michelangelo-like quality to the definition of his body, as though each muscle had been carved out of flesh-colored marble with a fine chisel.

Her eyes remained glued to his hands as he unbuckled his belt, unzipped his trousers and let the last of his clothing fall to the floor. He kicked off his shoes and stepped out of it all, taking a step toward the bed in all his naked glory.

"Well?" he asked after giving her a moment to take in every inch of the glorious sight. "Will I do?"

Gretchen laughed in a nervous titter. The man was beautiful, rock hard and very aroused. Any doubts she had about his attraction to her were instantly quelled. They were replaced by the anxiety of realizing he was a large specimen of man. She covered her nerves with a wide smile and a nod. "I suppose so."

One dark brow shot up at her blasé assessment of his manhood. Without responding, he approached the bed and reached for her waist. He gathered her dress and gave it a firm tug to slip it over her hips. When he dropped it to the floor, his gaze returned to her fully naked body.

Gretchen took a deep breath and fought the urge to cover herself. Instead she raised her hand and crooked her index finger to beckon him to her.

He didn't hesitate. Julian covered her body with his own, every inch of his blazing-hot skin touching hers.

The firm heat of him pressed at her thigh, urging her to open herself to him, so she did. He slipped between her legs and rested there. She could feel the tip of him teasing at her, but he didn't press forward. Not yet.

Instead, he hovered over her, lavishing more attention on her breasts. He kneaded and tasted her flesh, nipping at the tight peaks and flicking over them with his tongue until her back arched off the bed. Then, with one nipple drawn into his mouth, his hand slid down her stomach to delve between them. As he had at the chapel, his fingertips sought out her most sensitive flesh. He stroked over her in soft circles, building up another climax.

He slipped one finger inside her, stroking in and out of her tight body while his thumb still teased at her apex. The sensations coursing through her were so intense. She was desperate to keep her eyes open, yet no matter how hard she fought, they kept closing so she could savor the feeling.

He added a second finger, stretching her body wider and intensifying the ache in her belly. She easily accommodated him, anxious and ready for everything he had to offer.

That was when he pulled away. Gretchen's eyes flew open in time to see him reach for something beside the bed. A condom, she realized, as he quickly applied it and returned to the bed. As he moved across the mattress, his hands slipped behind her knees and bent them, drawing her legs up and spreading her wider for him.

Julian hovered over her then, watching her with a curious expression on his face. Then he lowered his face to hers and kissed her. Gretchen wrapped her arms around his neck and gave herself over to the kiss.

He rocked forward in short, slow strokes, rubbing the tip of his erection against her, picking up where his hands had left off a moment ago. She felt the orgasm building up inside her again. He sped up, rubbing over her sensitive flesh again and again as her cries escalated.

She was about to come a second time. She could feel the tension in her, about to break. "Julian," she gasped, clinging to his neck. "Yes, yes!" she cried out as she went over the edge.

That's when he entered her in one quick thrust. Pleasure. Pain. It was so fast, she almost didn't realize what had happened until it was done. She gasped with a mix of surprise and release as the last tremors of her orgasm traveled through her body.

Julian held himself remarkably still, even as he was buried deep inside her. His eyes were closed, a look of near pain on his face.

"Are you okay?" she asked.

His brows drew together as he looked down at her. "Aren't I supposed to be the one asking that question?"

"I suppose, but you're the one that looks like you're being hurt."

He shook his head. "Oh, it doesn't hurt. Not at all. I'm just trying to restrain myself a little."

Testing the waters, he eased out slowly and thrust forward again. Gretchen's body lit up with tiny pinpricks of sensation, most of them wonderful. "Don't. It's done. Now make love to me, Julian. Please."

With a curt nod, he shifted his weight and moved in her again with agonizing restraint. Now it was his turn to groan aloud. The feeling was amazing, but Gretchen couldn't help watching Julian's responses. She loved that she was able to give him pleasure, something she hadn't entirely considered before this moment.

Any residual soreness faded away as his movements came faster. Feeling more bold, she drew her knees up, cradling him between her thighs. The movement allowed him to move deeper, and she gasped as she adjusted to the feeling.

Julian swore against her cheek, a low rumble of approval that vibrated to her core. "You feel so amazing, but if you keep moving like that, I'm going to lose it."

"Lose it," she encouraged. She wanted him to lose control because of her. "Like you said earlier, we've got all night."

"Yes, we do."

Closing his eyes, Julian moved harder into her, the quick thrusts pushing him over the edge in mere minutes. His muscles tensed beneath the skin, his breath labored. She watched as he surged into her one last time, his jaw dropping open with a silent groan and shudder that ran through his whole body.

And then it was done. It was official. Gretchen was no longer a pathetic twenty-nine-year-old virgin. Julian rolled off onto his side and collapsed back against the bed with ragged breaths.

Gretchen could only lie there and smile as she gazed up at the ceiling. They'd just finished, and she couldn't wait to do it again.

A familiar sound roused Julian from his satiated sleep. One eye pried open to look at the screen on his cell phone as it charged on the nearby nightstand. It was the last number he wanted to see, especially at such an early hour, but it was the one he'd been anticipating all week. He'd had a feeling something wasn't quite right with his brother, and he was usually spot-on with that.

Shooting up in bed, he grabbed the phone and answered.

"Hello?" he said in a sleepy, gravelly voice.

"Mr. Curtis?" the woman said, using Julian's real last name.

"Yes?"

"Mr. Curtis, I'm sorry to call at such a late hour, but this is Theresa from the Hawthorne Community."

He knew that. He knew the minute he picked up the phone. Now get to the point. "Is James okay?"

A hesitation, slight but noticeable, preceded her answer. "He's stable," she said. "He's developed pneumonia and we're going to be transferring him to the hospital for observation."

Julian fought the confusing mix of sleep and panic. "Do I need to come? Is he going to be all right?"

"We don't think you need to come yet," Theresa said. "Right now he's stabilized. We're going to see how he reacts to treatment. He already has so much difficulty breathing, this just makes things that much harder for him."

"Yes, I know. Someone will call me as soon as there's a change?"

"Yes, Mr. Curtis. That's what James's file says, which is why we called you at such a late hour. You're to be notified any time there's a major medical change for him."

Julian nodded at the phone. That was the way he wanted it. If anything went wrong, he wanted to know. He couldn't be there with him, but he could make sure

James had all the best doctors and treatment that a movie star's salary could provide. "Thank you."

The call ended. Julian dropped the phone into his lap and took a deep breath to expel the fear that held his lungs captive. It was only fair—if James couldn't breathe, Julian shouldn't be able to breathe, either. That was never the way it was in reality. Julian was perfect. Healthy and able-bodied. James was not. The constant stream of late-night calls over the years had proven that much.

"Julian?" Gretchen's soft, concerned voice called to him from the pillows. "Is everything all right?"

A sudden feeling of dread, more powerful than the one that rushed over him as his phone rang, overcame Julian. Gretchen was in bed beside him. She'd heard everything. This situation had the potential to go horribly wrong.

"Uh, yeah," he said dismissively, hoping she would let it go. Very few people in his life knew about James's situation. Hell, almost no one knew about James at all. Julian kept it that way on purpose. He certainly didn't need the press exploiting this story. James had never asked for anyone's pity, and making him a headline could potentially have millions of people looking at his brother as though there was something wrong with him. He didn't want that. Despite everything, James had always just wanted to live a normal life. Being at the Hawthorne Community had given him that. He had his own apartment, his own helper and a staff of professionals to care for him when he needed it. Julian didn't want to ruin that for his brother.

Gretchen sat up beside him in bed and leaned her

bare shoulder against him. "For an actor, you're not a very good liar."

Julian chuckled softly. "Three a.m. is not the peak hour for my craft, I suppose." He turned to her, planted a soft kiss on her lips and ignored the concern in her eyes. "It's nothing. You can go back to sleep."

He expected her to lie down, but instead he felt her arm wrap around his shoulders. "Julian, I told you my secret and you were able to…uh…help me out. Tell me what's going on and maybe I can help you in return."

He shook his head. "Gretchen, if this was as simple as making love to you, I'd tell you in a second. But this can't be fixed by you or anyone else." Julian returned his phone to the charger and lay down in the hopes she would do the same.

She did, pressing her naked body against his and resting her head on his chest. Normally, thoughts of desire would've rushed through his mind and he would've made love to her again, but there were too many worries in his mind now.

"Tell me," Gretchen said. "It's dark. We're both half asleep. You don't have to look at me while you say it. Just get it off your chest. You'll feel better."

Julian had never told anyone about this situation aside from Ross and the people who were a part of his life before he became a star, like Murray. Ross needed to know why he was so driven. But tonight, under the cover of darkness, he wanted to tell Gretchen the truth. She wasn't like those other women, mining for a story they could sell. If there was one person he could tell, it would be her. He didn't want to keep it from her.

"My brother is in the hospital," he said simply.

"I'm sorry to hear that. Is it serious?"

"Unfortunately, everything is serious when it comes to my brother." That was true. A run-of-the-mill cold could be near fatal, much less the pneumonia he currently had.

"Tell me," she pressed again.

He wanted to, but he had to be careful. "If I do, you have to swear that you'll never tell a single soul what I've said. It's absolutely critical that no one know about this."

"Okay," she said. "You have my word."

Somehow, Julian knew that Gretchen wouldn't spill his secrets, but he had to put it out there and let her know how serious it all was. "I have an identical twin brother named James."

"I didn't realize you had a brother, much less an identical twin."

"No one knows. I try to keep my life before I went to Hollywood very quiet for my family's sake. They didn't ask for this spotlight to be shone on them. And since my brother has so many issues, I'm all the more protective of him."

"What's wrong with him?"

Julian sighed. There were so many things. James had never had a chance to live the truly normal life he wanted, no matter how hard they tried or how many specialists they brought in to see him. "My brother has a severe case of spastic cerebral palsy. The doctors said that he sustained some kind of brain injury in utero or during his birth that impaired his ability to function."

Gretchen didn't respond. He wasn't sure if she was surprised by his tale or wanted to let him just get it all off his chest.

"He was diagnosed when we were about two. My mom was in denial, thinking he was just slower to crawl and get around than I was, as though the two minutes older I was than James made that big of a difference. She finally took him to the doctor when she couldn't ignore the disparity any longer. The diagnosis was devastating, but the hardest part was not knowing how it would fully impact him until he got older. The severity of cerebral palsy can vary widely based on the injury. Some people can live normal, long lives with only a few limitations. My mother hoped for that, but by the time we were getting ready to start kindergarten and his problems became more pronounced, it was easy to see that it was getting harder for her to stay positive. She cried a lot when she thought I wasn't looking. James was wheelchair-bound and needed constant supervision. He had an aide at school that stayed with him and helped him through his day.

"The medical bills were crippling. Even though my father had a good job at a nearby production facility with solid benefits, it didn't cover everything. James went through so many surgeries and treatments. Hours of therapy and trips to the emergency room. Cerebral palsy doesn't get worse, you see. But the complications can. He'd had trouble swallowing and breathing since he was a baby. James nearly choked to death a couple times, and every time cold and flu season came around, we lived like a quarantine facility to keep him from catching anything. Eventually, when he was about ten, they had to put in a tracheostomy tube.

"As we got older, it got harder. James wasn't a little boy anymore—he was a growing teenager. Simple things like getting him out of his chair and into bed, or giving him a bath, got so difficult. We got a home health nurse to help out when we were in high school, but by the time I went off to college, Mom just couldn't handle it anymore. He had a really severe bout of pneumonia and he ended up in the hospital. The doctors told us that he needed better care than we could provide, and they recommended we put him in a state facility that was better equipped to handle James's treatment."

Finally, Gretchen spoke. "That must've been a very hard decision for your parents. Hard on all of you."

"You have no idea. I've lived my whole life with this guilt."

"Guilt? Why would you feel guilty? You didn't do anything wrong."

Julian stroked his hand over Gretchen's soft curls. "I was healthy. I was everything James wasn't. We were identical, we started absolutely the same in every way, and yet something went wrong—something I could've caused before we were even born. It's very easy to feel guilty."

"Did the doctors ever say that? Did they ever directly blame you for it?"

He shrugged. "If they did, my mother would never tell me. It wouldn't matter, though. I was still active and went out with friends and did all the things he couldn't do. When I went off to college and he went into a state hospital, the disparities were painful. And then my father died my junior year of college. In addition to our grief, we had to cope with the fact that now the family had no income and no insurance. My father's life insurance policy was barely enough to pay off the mortgage so my mother wasn't homeless. Something had to be done, so I dropped out of school and moved to LA."

"Really?"

"Stupid, right? I was convinced that I would go out

there and get acting work and be able to support my family. I could've just as easily landed a long-term role as a waiter who couldn't afford his own rent. But I met Ross. He saw potential in me. He might be a jerk sometimes, but he got me into some commercials, then small roles in movies. The next thing I knew, my parts were getting larger, and then I was offered a lead role. I wasn't an overnight success, but it only took a few years before I started making seven figures on a film. I wasn't thrilled with the parts, but they allowed me to move James to a private residential facility that specializes in patients with cerebral palsy. I was able to buy private health insurance for all of us and send my mom money to live on. I'd achieved my goal."

"That's why," Gretchen said with an enlightened tone.

"Why what?"

"Why you don't want to take those other roles. You said you worried about screwing up and damaging your career. It has nothing to do with your ego and everything to do with supporting your family."

Julian sighed. "Yes. They depend on me. I can't, won't, do anything to risk my career. Or to risk anyone finding out about James and turning him into a tabloid headline." As he said the words, he realized just by telling Gretchen this story, he'd compromised his brother. She might not mean to tell, but things could happen. If Ross knew, he'd insist on a confidentiality agreement. Not exactly his usual pillow talk, but he supposed everything was different with Gretchen.

"I know I made you promise not to tell anyone, but to tie up loose ends and ensure my brother's protection, I'll probably need to have Ross draft up a confidentiality agreement in the morning. I know he'll insist on it. I'll also see to it that he adds another five thousand to your payment to compensate for your cooperation. It's not your fault I dumped this on you."

He felt Gretchen stiffen beneath his fingertips, and then she raised her head to look at him. "Are you serious?"

Julian frowned. "This is the way my life works. Contracts and compensation, even in my personal life."

She just watched him for a moment, but her body remained stiff as a board. Finally, she said, "I'll sign your stupid agreement, Julian." The tone of her voice was sharp. He could tell he'd offended her. "But I'm not taking any more of your money."

Eight

Any second now, someone was going to wake Gretchen up. She sat in front of her vanity applying her makeup the way the woman at the department store had told her to. Draped across the bed behind her was the gown she was wearing to the wedding as Julian's date. That was surreal enough on its own. Knowing she'd slept with him the night before was completely in the dream realm.

She'd waited years for that moment, never once anticipating that she would end up in the arms of one of the sexiest men alive. Gretchen still couldn't quite understand why he wanted her. It annoyed him when she mentioned it, so she'd stopped. But even if she'd had a healthy sense of self-esteem going into this scenario, it would be unbelievable.

The only thing about the past few days that convinced Gretchen that all of this was real was their awkward discussion after his call about James. She had been high on the excitement of having sex for the first time and thrilled that Julian was willing to share something that personal with her. Then he started talking about confidentiality contracts and worse—paying her to keep quiet about it.

The longer they were together, the easier it was for her to forget that none of this was real and that she was being compensated for her time. She hadn't liked the idea of this from the beginning, but as they went on, she liked it even less. With sex added to the mix, she was starting to feel very *Pretty Woman* about the whole thing. The additional money for her silence just rubbed salt in the wound and reminded her that she was that much closer to being a whore.

"Ugh," she said as she applied the last of her mascara and threw it down onto the table in disgust. She needed to get out of here and distract herself with the chaos of the wedding so she didn't stew in those thoughts any longer.

Looking into the mirror, she admired her handiwork. It wasn't bad at all. She'd already straightened her hair and wrapped it into a French twist with a crystal barrette securing it. Having her hair up made her neck look longer and her face look thinner, which was great. She anticipated a lot of cameras being around today since it was the big event they'd been building up to. She had to be believable as Julian's girlfriend, and a double chin wouldn't help her case at all.

With her undergarments in place, Gretchen slipped into the gown she'd chosen with Amelia. It was strapless with a sweetheart neckline and a high waist that fell right under her bust. The top was a shiny black ruched satin, but below the waist, it was flowing white satin, painted in purple, blue and black almost like a wearable piece of watercolor art. It was beautiful and fit her perfectly.

The last piece she added was the necklace Julian had given her. The fiery opal rested nicely on the bare expanse of her chest, falling right below her collarbone.

Admiring herself in the full-length mirror on her closet door, she was stunned by what she saw. This wasn't the mousy, awkward Gretchen from a week ago. She looked confident, radiant and even beautiful. Gretchen was ready to walk out the door and be Julian's girl, which was a good thing, because it was time to go. She needed to get back to the facility.

It felt weird enough already that she wasn't there helping the others, but she'd done her part, including buzzing by this morning to meet the florist and snatch up those wayward panties. Now she was returning as a guest. Since Julian was the best man, he wasn't able to pick her up. He was in the groom's room, likely doing a shot of whiskey with Murray and helping him with his tie. They had to be ready early so Bree could take pictures of the wedding party before the ceremony.

Just in case, Gretchen threw a few last things into an overnight bag she'd packed. If she did end up staying with Julian again, she wanted to be ready and not slink back home in the morning in a gown. She had all her toiletries, a change of clothes and a slinky little red lace chemise that had been rotting in her closet since she'd impulse-purchased it several years back. She was looking forward to someone actually seeing her in it, aside from her.

After loading everything into her car, she returned

to the chapel. Gathered on the curb outside the facility was a crowd of photographers. The location had leaked, as expected, but they weren't allowed on the grounds. With very little activity outside with the winter weather, all they'd get were shots of people coming in and out. They paid little attention to her in her cheap sedan. She was able to slip in the back door as usual.

"Wow."

Gretchen paused outside her office where she was about to stow her overnight bag. Turning, she saw Natalie watching her from the hallway. She was all geared up with her headset, her tablet and fierce determination to tackle the day, but the expression of awe on her face was new.

"Do I look okay?"

Natalie nodded, coming close to admire the dress. "You look amazing. Every bit the girlfriend of a movie star, no doubt."

Gretchen beamed. She thought she looked nice, but was nice good enough? It seemed so, at least in Natalie's opinion.

"I especially like the well-bedded glow. Is that a bronzer or an all-night lovemaking session?"

Gretchen's eyes widened and she brought her hand to her lips to shush her. "Bronzer," she said pointedly. "We'll discuss the brand and how well it was applied later."

Natalie gave her a wicked grin and swung her dark ponytail over her shoulder. "You bet we will. The ballroom looks great, so relax and have fun today."

"I'll try." Gretchen put her things into her office, then went around the facility checking on a few last-minute things. All was well in the ballroom. The pin lights were perfect, and the floral arrangements added the ideal touch. Amelia's wedding cake was an eight-tier masterpiece nestled in a bed of white pastillage roses. All that was left was for the servers to light the candles and the guests to mill in.

She crossed the lobby and found Julian, Murray and the other groomsmen in the chapel taking photos with Bree and another guy who was probably from the magazine that had the exclusive to the event. Gretchen couldn't help the wide smile on her face when her eyes met Julian's, especially when his own smile returned her excitement. He looked so handsome in his tuxedo, as if he were auditioning to be the next James Bond. And he was hers, at least for now. Their relationship might be short, but it was special, and she'd always think of it that way.

Natalie followed her into the chapel, this time on official planner duties. "Okay, gentlemen, we need to get all of you except the ushers back into the gentlemen's suite. The guests are about to arrive. Ushers, please meet me back here so we can go over your instructions one last time."

The men filed out, Julian pressing a kiss to her cheek as he went by, so as not to mess up her lipstick. "I'll meet you in the lobby after these two get hitched."

"I'll be waiting," she said, trying out a seductive smile. She wasn't entirely sure that it worked, but Julian sighed and reluctantly followed Murray out of the chapel. That was proof enough for her.

"All right," Natalie shouted. "Ushers at the doors. Musicians, please cue up the string medley to take us through to the groom's entrance. Gretchen…do something with yourself. Let one of the ushers seat you. They need practice." Without another word, she disappeared from the room.

As she was told, Gretchen returned to the entrance and approached one of the ushers with a polite smile.

"Are you a guest of the bride or the groom?"

"The groom."

He nodded, handed her one of the programs she'd made and took her arm to lead her down the aisle and to a seat on the right side of the chapel. She wasn't alone for long. Guests started arriving in huge waves. This was a big wedding, putting the facility's capacity limits to the test. Every spot in the parking lot, every seat in the chapel, would be taken, and taken by Nashville royalty.

The room filled quickly. Gretchen tried not to act out of place as different country music stars were seated around her. Before long, the chapel looked like the audience at the Country Music Awards. She was pretty certain Garth Brooks and Trisha Yearwood were sitting right behind her. It was odd, but that hadn't fazed her when she was working—a guest was a guest—but as a guest herself, it felt extremely bizarre to be sitting among them. She had to keep reminding herself that her date was a movie star and she needed to be cool.

The string quartet's music medley faded, and she recognized them changing to the song they played when the parents were escorted in, then the officiant and the groomsmen entered. Julian sought her out in the crowd and gave her a sly wink as he went by. It was enough to make her heart flutter in her chest.

They assembled on the raised platform, and the music announced the arrival of the bridesmaids, then Kelly with her father. Gretchen stood with the crowd as the bride walked down the aisle in a lace-and-crystal extravaganza, custom-made for a country music diva.

As the wedding began, Gretchen felt her mind stray. Her gaze drifted to Julian, standing by with the ring and to catch Murray if he fainted. He looked so calm, so natural, compared to Murray, who'd started to sweat and could barely make it through his vows his voice was shaking so badly. Of course, Julian wasn't the one getting married.

She imagined he'd still be calm at his own wedding. Even if he felt nervous, he'd fall back on his actor training and play the part of a confident groom. He'd speak the words to her without faltering, with nothing but love and adoration on his face and in his voice…

Oh, no. She stopped herself. Gretchen might be in the midst of a lusty haze, but she wasn't letting herself go *there*. She wasn't a naive girl who thought the man who took her virginity would love her forever and marry her and they'd live happily ever after. She knew the truth and she'd accepted it, despite the ridiculous tangent her brain had taken. Like it or not, she was a paid companion. He wouldn't be looking adoringly at her and speaking vows of any kind, ever.

With a sigh, Gretchen let her gaze drop into her lap as she pretended to study the program. Maybe it was a good thing that their time together was coming to an end. Keeping her heart out of the arrangement with Julian was getting harder and harder.

He needed to get on that plane back to Beverly Hills before she lost the fight.

Julian couldn't wait for the ceremony and all the pictures to be over so he could hold Gretchen in his arms again. She'd hovered on the fringes during the photo shoot, watching with adoration in her eyes, as she was instructed.

Their progressing physical relationship had certainly made their public appearances easier. Neither of them really had to act anymore. They just did what felt natural and it translated beautifully. He'd already had several people ask him about Gretchen, and he couldn't help boasting about how smart and talented and beautiful she was.

It was all true.

At last, Julian's duties were over, save for his toast at the reception. The wedding party finally made their way over to the ballroom and took their places to welcome the happy couple and witness their first dance. That done, they were allowed to take their seats, eat their dinner and finally relax. The round of toasts was completed during the salad course, effectively allowing Julian to be off duty the rest of the night. Weddings were exhausting, almost a bigger production than some of the movies he'd starred in.

"You look amazing," he leaned in and said to Gretchen as the wedding cake was served. Julian wasn't interested in dessert. He had a hard time tearing his eyes away from the exposed line of her neck and shoulders. He ached to run his fingertip along her bare skin and leave a line of kisses in its wake.

Gretchen smiled at his assessment, her cheeks blushing adorably. "Thank you. You're looking pretty dapper yourself."

"Meh." He dismissed it. He wasn't interested in talking about himself tonight. He wanted the focus to be on her. "I can't wait to get you out on the dance floor and show you off to everyone."

Gretchen stiffened slightly, looking at him with concern in her dark eyes. "Dancing? We've never discussed the subject of dancing before. I've got a lovely pair of two left feet."

"You can't be that bad," he dismissed.

"No, you don't understand. My mother was a professionally trained ballerina. She tried to teach me to dance for years, then finally declared I was about as elegant and graceful as a rhino in heels."

Julian flinched. That was a horrible thing to say to someone, much less your own daughter. No wonder she'd gone this long thinking she wasn't worthy of a man's attentions. "We're not doing that kind of dancing," he insisted. "I'm going to hold you close and we'll just lose ourselves in the music. Nothing fancy, just dance floor foreplay."

"Foreplay?" Her arched brow raised curiously.

"You betcha." Julian knew a lot of guys didn't like to dance, but those guys were damn fools. If they only knew how a good slow dance could prime the pumps, they'd all sign up for ballroom dancing lessons.

As if on cue, the bandleader invited the whole wedding party out onto the dance floor. "Here's our chance," he said.

"Aren't you supposed to dance with the maid of honor?"

He turned to see her step out onto the floor with another man. "I guess not. Would you care to help a lonely gentleman out?"

Gretchen nervously took his hand and let him lead her out onto the dance floor. The song was slow and romantic, allowing him to take full advantage of the moment. He slipped his arms around her waist, pulling her close. It took a minute for her to relax, but eventually, she put her arms around his neck and took a deep breath to release the tension.

"See? This isn't so bad."

"You're right. And if it wasn't for the frantic flashing of cameras taking pictures, I might be able to relax."

Julian shrugged. He'd learned long ago to tune all that out. It was hard for an actor to stay in the moment if he couldn't ignore the camera in his face, the lights shining on him and the boom mike hanging overhead. There were really only two photographers tonight; the rest were just guests taking photos like at any other wedding. They were harmless.

"This moment is what the whole week was about. Let them take their pictures. Let them plaster it across their celebrity gossip magazine pages and make you a household name if that's the price for bringing you into my life."

Gretchen gasped softly at his bold words. He'd surprised himself with the intensity of them, but it had felt right at the moment. As time went on, he realized that he just couldn't let this go when he returned home. He didn't know how they could manage it or if it would work at all, but he wanted to try. He would be a fool to let such a sweet, caring woman drift out of his life.

The moment was perfect, like one carefully crafted by one of his directors. The lighting was dim with the occasional beam dancing across them. The music was soft and seductive, their bodies moving in time with it. Every inch of her soft curves was pressed against him. When she laid her head on his shoulder, it was as if the world had ceased to exist. The wedding guests, the cameras…all of it felt as if it was suddenly a million miles away and they were dancing all alone.

Her touch made his skin prickle with sensations,

but none could come close to the lightness inside him. With Gretchen in his arms, he felt as though he could do anything. He could take on that gritty script, he could pursue a more serious acting career without compromising his brother's care, he could have everything he wanted...including her.

It had been only a few days, but he had Gretchen to thank for opening his eyes to the possibilities. He intended to talk to Ross about it tomorrow morning. That script was everything he wanted, and a part of him needed to try out for it. He might not get it, or he might wish he hadn't when the critics got a hold of him, but he needed to try.

The song came to an end, and Julian could feel the spell drift away with the last notes. This night could only be more perfect with Gretchen in his bed again. He wanted to get out of here before something interfered.

"Are you ready to go, Cinderella?" he asked as he led her off the dance floor.

"I don't know," she said with a wrinkled nose. "The minute we step out the door, it's over, isn't it? Our little fantasy relationship turns back into a pumpkin at midnight. If leaving means it's over, then no. I want to stay and dance until the band unplugs and goes home."

Julian pulled her tight against him and kissed her. A tingle traveled straight to his toes, making his feet feel as though they were asleep. "I'm not sure what time period Ross negotiated, but I really don't care. If we walk out of this ballroom, I intend to take you back to my hotel and make love to you all night. And I'm going to keep doing that until I have to get on a plane and go back to LA. I don't know about you, but to me, what's going on between us has nothing to do with any business arrangement."

"It's not for me, either."

Julian smiled. "Then slip out of this ballroom with me right now."

Gretchen looked around the dim ballroom at the crowd on the dance floor and the others milling around their tables. "Isn't it too early to leave? Isn't there anything else you need to do as the best man?"

Julian shook his head. "I'm done. We'll see them tomorrow morning at the farewell brunch."

She was biting her lip, but he could tell he'd won the battle by the naughty glint in her eye. "Okay, let me go get my bag out of my office and we can go."

Julian took Gretchen's hand and they made their way out of the ballroom. He was moving quickly, weaving through the other guests. He couldn't wait to peel that dress off her tonight. In the lobby, he waited while she dashed down the hallway to grab her things.

Then he heard it: the special ringtone designated for his brother's care facility. Reaching into his tuxedo pocket, he grabbed his phone and said a silent prayer.

"Hello?" he said, wishing the voice on the line would tell him it was a wrong number or something.

"Mr. Curtis?" the woman said, dashing his hopes. "Yes?"

"Mr. Curtis, I'm sorry to have to call again, but this is Theresa from the Hawthorne Community. James's condition has gotten substantially worse since we spoke last."

"He's in the hospital, isn't he?"

"Yes, but he isn't responding quickly enough to treatment. The doctors think they might have to put him on a ventilator to keep his oxygen levels high enough while the pneumonia clears up."

Julian should know more about his brother's condition and what all this would mean for him, but he didn't. His brother's tracheostomy was supposed to solve his breathing problems, but apparently it wasn't enough this time. "What does that mean? Is he going to be okay?"

"We don't know. We called to give you the status and let you know that your mother is with him and hopes you can come as well. Do you think that will be possible?"

"Yes, I'm in Nashville right now. I can be there in a few hours. Which hospital is he staying in?"

"He's at the university hospital. I'll be sure to let your mother know you're on your way."

"Thank you. Goodbye."

Julian hung up the phone and slipped it back into his pocket. He looked over his shoulder as Gretchen came from her office with her purse and a small duffel bag.

"Gretchen…" He stopped. He hated to derail everything, but he had no choice. "I'm going to have to cancel on tonight. I just got a call about James and I'm leaving for Kentucky as soon as I walk out of here."

Her dark eyes widened with concern lining them. "Is he going to be okay?"

Julian felt a tightness constrict his chest, making it almost impossible for him to get out the words. "I… don't know. I just know that I have to go. I'm so sorry. This isn't how I wanted tonight to end."

"Then let's not let it end. Let's go."

"Go?" he asked in confusion. "You mean you want to go to Kentucky with me?"

She nodded quickly, without hesitation. "Absolutely." Walking up to Julian, she placed a reassuring kiss on his lips and then took his hand to tug him toward the door. "Let's get on the road."

Nine

Julian hated hospitals. A lot of his childhood had been spent in one while his brother was tested and treated. Julian was the lucky one—no one ever came after him with needles and scalpels—but the scent when they exited the elevator was unmistakable. Bleach and blood and God-knows-what-else.

Having a firm grip on Gretchen's hand made it easier. He'd never considered bringing her here until she suggested it, and then he'd realized he didn't want it any other way. For all his muscles, having her here made him feel stronger. He wanted to introduce her to his family; he wanted to share this secretive part of his life with someone.

As they approached the waiting room outside the ICU, he heard his mother's voice calling to him. Turning, he saw her pick up the coffee she was making and head their way.

His mother had been—and in his eyes still was—
a beautiful woman. Time and stress had aged her faster
than they should've, but you could still see the sparkle
of the vibrant young woman beneath it all. Her wavy
dark hair was more gray than brown anymore, but she
still had the same bright smile, and her blue-gray eyes
lit up when she saw him. Julian had her eyes, his own
color much more sedate without his colored contacts.

"I'm so glad you could make it." She smiled as she
approached, wrapping him in a big hug, then turning to
look at his unexpected companion. "And who is this?"

"I'm Gretchen," she said, reaching out to take the
woman's hand. "It's nice to meet you, Mrs. Cooper."

His mother smiled and shook her head. "It's Curtis,
dear. Cooper is Julian's stage name. You can just call
me Denise."

"Mom, Gretchen and I are seeing each other." It may
have only been for a week, but it was true. This was
more than just a setup relationship to him.

His mother looked them both up and down. "We've
interrupted something important, haven't we? You two
look like you came here straight from an awards show
or something."

"Just a wedding that was winding down anyway,"
Julian insisted. "You remember Murray, my roommate
in college?"

She nodded. "Oh, yes, I bought one of his albums
for James to listen to. That explains why you were in
Nashville. Convenient timing, although there's never
really a good time for this." His mother smoothed over
her hair, which was pulled back into a bun.

"How is he doing?"

She shrugged, drawing her oversize cardigan tighter

around her. "It changes by the hour. Doctors keep waiting, hoping his blood oxygen levels will start coming back up without further intervention, but they could decide to go ahead and put him on the ventilator. They worry that if they take that step, he might be on it permanently. I just hate it. He was doing so well."

His mother shook her head sadly. "That trip to Europe for the Botox treatments made a huge difference. He was able to stretch his legs out, and the casts corrected some of the alignment problems he had in his legs. We were hopeful that with enough therapy we might get him walking, but this will set him back again. He's always had the breathing troubles."

Over the years, the spastic nature of his brother's cerebral palsy had worsened as his underutilized muscles started to atrophy. He'd undergone multiple surgeries and years of therapy to lengthen his muscles in the hopes he could walk or manage other dexterity tasks on his own, but they always drew back up. The controversial Botox treatments weren't legal in the States, but they'd taken the risk and traveled to a doctor who could try it. It had cost a fortune, but James had done so well afterward, it had been worth every penny.

"Can we see him?"

His mother bit at her bottom lip, reminding him of Gretchen. "Visiting hours are over, but maybe we can talk to someone." His mother disappeared, returning a few minutes later with an encouraging smile on her face. "They're going to let the two of you go back now, but just for five or ten minutes. You'll have to come back again in the morning. He's in the bed at the far end of the unit on the right. I'll wait here for you and drink some more coffee. It's going to be a long night for me."

"Okay, we'll be out in a minute." Julian hugged his mother, then led Gretchen with him through the double doors of the ICU. They walked around the nurse's station and to the end of the hall. Taking a deep breath, he pushed back the curtain and found his identical twin lying in a hospital bed. It was such a familiar sight, he almost didn't react to it the way he should've. His brother's eyes fluttered open, then a lopsided smile spread across his face.

"Julian," he mouthed with a raspy whisper, breaking into a fit of coughing.

"Try not to talk too much, James. Use your signs." He let go of Gretchen's hand to walk to his brother's bedside. He scooped up James's clenched fist and patted it. Both the boys had learned sign language when they were young to help James communicate without speaking. It was helpful when the tracheostomy made it that much more difficult for him to speak. "Mom says you're having trouble breathing. Have you been sneaking pot again?"

His brother smiled at his joke and shook his head. "Can't get any. Mean nurses," he signed. James took a few rattling, wheezing lungfuls of air through the tracheostomy tube in his throat, making Julian more worried the longer he stood there.

Most people with a tracheostomy could speak by covering the tube with their finger or chin. Because James had such limited control of his hands and arms, that hadn't been an option for him. Instead, they'd adjusted the valve in his windpipe so he could get just enough air to whisper between breaths. Even then, his speech was limited by muscle control in his throat and face. He tended to sign most of the time to get his point across, but occasionally, he'd speak a few words. It had never taken much for Julian to understand him. They were identical twins; Julian knew his brother inside and out. He just couldn't help him.

"James, this is my friend Gretchen. She wanted to meet you."

James's head was almost always cocked unnaturally to the side with a pillow supporting his neck, but his gaze traveled past his brother to Gretchen. His left arm was drawn to his chest, but he waved his fingers at her. "Pretty," he signed.

"Yes, she is. She's very pretty."

"I'd hit that," James whispered with a smile.

Julian and Gretchen both broke into unexpected laughter. Despite everything, James always had a sense of humor. Whatever trauma that had impacted his ability to control his body had left his cognitive powers intact. He was smart and funny, and it made Julian sad that the world would miss out on what James could've done if he'd been born healthy like his brother.

"Uh, thank you, James," she said, blushing at his amusing compliment. "How are you feeling?"

James shrugged. His brother probably didn't know what it was like to feel good. He had okay days and bad days, but even his best days could be hard on him. Those were the days when he felt well enough to think about how he was trapped in a body that couldn't do what he wanted it to do.

A loud, wheezing breath rattled through James's trach tube, but it was quickly drowned out by a shrill beeping noise that sounded from the machine by James's bed. Julian looked up, noting that the blood oxygen percentage on the screen was blinking red.

The nurse came in a second later, checking the screens.

"You two will have to leave. We've got to get the ventilator hooked up."

Two other nurses and a resident came in behind her, and Julian was pushed out into the hallway with Gretchen. As he watched them work on his brother, Julian realized that his fantasies of doing serious films were just that—fantasies. Hard-hitting, low-budget indie films might reap all the awards and get the buzz at Sundance, but they wouldn't pay these bills. They wouldn't cover charter flights to Europe for experimental treatments. Giving James the absolute best quality of life was his number one priority. His vanity and his artistic needs would always take second place to that.

"We'd better go," Gretchen said, tugging at his arm.

Reluctantly, he followed her out of the ICU, dreading the news he'd have to share with his mother in the waiting room. The woman hadn't gotten a stitch of good news in almost thirty years. He hated to pile more on top of it.

But he knew that with the news would be his promise that he'd take care of it. Just as he always had. And always would.

They stumbled into a Louisville hotel room near the hospital at almost three in the morning. Gretchen was exhausted down to her bones, and yet too much had happened for her to sleep anytime soon. She could tell Julian was feeling the same way after how he'd paced in the hotel lobby while they got a room. Even if they went straight to bed, they'd both likely lie there with their brains spinning.

Gretchen flipped on the lights of their suite, revealing a tasteful and modern room. It had a separate sitting area from the bedroom, like Julian's room in Nashville. He carried her bag into the bedroom and laid it out on the bed. They'd left in such a rush, he didn't have a bag of his own. All he'd had was a small leather travel case he'd taken with him to the wedding chapel with things he might need throughout the day.

Now he stood at the foot of the bed, silently tugging off his bow tie and slipping out of his tuxedo jacket. She could tell he was distracted and worried about James. Gretchen knew that if one of her sisters were in the hospital, she'd be beside herself.

Instead of watching him undress, she took her bag into the bathroom to change. She'd spent far too many hours in this strapless bra, and she was ready to be done with it all. Unzipping her bag, she looked inside and groaned. Unfortunately, when she'd packed, she'd packed for a sexy night at his hotel. A detour to Louisville to see his sick brother hadn't been on the radar. The only pajamas she had were of the sexy red lace variety. With the dark cloud looming over Julian, she doubted he would be interested.

But with limited options, she slipped into the chemise and pulled the fluffy hotel bathrobe over it. When she returned to the bedroom, Julian's suit was lying across the chair and he was gone. She found him in the living room, standing in front of the minibar clad in just a pair of boxer briefs as he held a tumbler of golden liquid in his hand. Scotch, she'd guess.

"You're drinking?" she asked. That was the first thing she'd seen him drink aside from water since they met.

"Yeah," he said, looking thoughtfully at the glass. "My trainer can punish me later. That's the beauty of being able-bodied. I just… I just needed something to numb all the feelings inside me. A bottle of water and a protein bar wasn't going to do it."

Gretchen nodded. She hated to see him like this, but there wasn't much she could do. Instead, she sat down on the couch and beckoned him to sit beside her. He slammed back the rest of his drink and left it on the counter before he came over and collapsed onto the pillows.

Without saying anything, Gretchen snuggled up beside him. He wrapped his arm around her shoulder and hugged her tight against him.

"I want to talk about something other than my brother," he said after a long silence. "Tell me…" Julian hesitated. "Tell me about how someone so beautiful and full of life could be so awkward and inexperienced with men."

Really? That was the last topic she wanted to discuss, but if it would take his mind off James, she would confess it all. With her face buried against his chest, she started the not-so-interesting tale of her life. "My mother was a ballerina. She toured with a company for several years before she broke her ankle and retired. She met my father, a physical therapist, while she was doing rehab on her leg. She was tall and willowy, educated in the classics, and he was shorter and stockier, with more knowledge about football than anything else, but for some reason, they hit it off.

"They married and had three girls. I was the middle child. My sisters were always so much like my mother, so graceful and so skilled when it came to charming men. I took after my father. I was always chubby, always clumsy. I actually got kicked out of kinder ballet classes because I kept knocking over the other children. To say I was a disappointment to my mother was an understatement."

"Did she actually say that to you? That you were a disappointment?"

"No. But she always pushed me to be more like my sisters. She didn't seem to understand me at all. Even if I hadn't been stockier or uncoordinated, I was very shy. I was much more comfortable with my art and my books than with boys. I really didn't have much in common with anyone in my family. And when I got old enough to date, I don't know, I guess I sabotaged myself. I didn't feel pretty, I didn't feel confident and so guys never noticed me. I was so quiet, I could virtually fade into the background, unseen and unheard. It just continued on like that and after a while, I decided that maybe I was meant to be one of those suffering artists, destined to be alone."

"That's ridiculous." Julian eased back and lifted her chin with his finger until she had no choice but to look him in the eye. "There's no way a woman like you would end up alone. You're beautiful, talented, smart, passionate... You've got way too much to offer a man. He just has to be smart enough to see you when others don't. I'll admit that I probably wouldn't have been that guy. I'm always on the move, always too distracted to see things that aren't right in front of my face. And if Ross hadn't set up this date, I would've missed out on a wonderful few days because of my blindness."

Gretchen felt the blush of embarrassment rise to her cheeks. She wanted to pull away, to avoid his gaze, but he wouldn't let her.

"I mean it. You don't know how much it meant to

have you here with me tonight. I'm always the one that comes in to save the day. It was nice, for once, to have someone to hold my hand, to support me when I needed it. It's so hard watching James's health deteriorate, but having you there made all the difference."

"I'm glad I could be there. No one should have to go through that alone."

His blue eyes focused on hers, and she noticed for the first time that he'd taken out his contact lenses. The stunning Caribbean blue eyes she was used to looking at were now the soft blue-gray of the northern seas. The color suited him more, and she liked seeing him without part of his Hollywood facade. "Your eyes are a beautiful color," she said.

"They don't pop on camera," he said, deflating her compliment.

"That's the camera's loss."

He watched her for a moment before he spoke. "Gretchen, I don't want this to end."

The surprise shift in the conversation threw her off and she sat up, pulling away from him and taking a few seconds to respond appropriately. "Neither do I, but what choice do we have? You're going back to LA, and my business and my life are in Nashville."

He nodded in agreement, but he had a firm set in his jaw that told her he wasn't giving up that easily. "It would be complicated, yes, but I want to try. I can't just walk away from you like this. Say you want to be with me—no contracts, no faking it for the cameras."

Gretchen almost couldn't believe her ears. He was serious. He wanted to be with her, truly be with her, and not just because his manager was behind it or they were enjoying the benefits of their arrangement. A woman like her being with a man like Julian was some kind of fantasy come to life. How could she say no to that, especially when just a look from him could make her chest so tight she could barely breathe? She certainly wasn't looking forward to letting Julian go. She'd tried to keep her heart out of this short-term scenario, but with every minute that ticked by, she was losing the fight. Was it really possible that she wouldn't have to give him up when his plane took off on Monday?

"I want to be with you, Julian," she said, and she meant it. "I don't know how we'd manage, but I don't want to let this go, either."

"Then don't." Julian leaned into her and pressed his lips against hers. He kept advancing, easing her back until she was lying on the cushions of the couch. His hands fumbled with the tie of her belt, opening the robe and pulling back to admire what was beneath it.

"Holy hell," he said, running his fingers over the red satin-and-lace chemise. "You've had this on the whole time?"

"Just since we got here."

"And we've been talking? If I'd known what you had under that robe, we could've found some more pleasurable distractions than talking."

His lips met hers. Unlike the night before, there was less tenderness in his touch. There was a tension there, and she knew it was stress. He needed a distraction, and she was happy to be that for him tonight. She wanted him to lose himself in her and forget about all his troubles.

His hand glided up her outer thigh, pushing the robe out of the way and brushing against the lace edges of her negligee. "Did you know," he asked, as his hand ran across her stomach, caressing her through the fabric, "that red is my favorite color?"

Gretchen smiled, parting her legs for him to draw closer. "Is it really?"

"It is now." He punctuated the words by burying his face in her neck. He tugged at the plunging neckline of her nightie until her breasts were exposed and he could tease at them with his rough palms.

She still hadn't quite adjusted to the idea that she was a sexually active woman now. She still felt as though she was fumbling around, but being with Julian made it so easy. All she had to do was close her eyes and do whatever felt right. So far, that hadn't steered her wrong, and Julian certainly seemed to like it.

Drawing her leg up, she hooked it around his hip, pulling his firm desire closer to the slip of satin that separated them. Julian groaned when they made contact, rubbing himself across her most sensitive spot. The tiny panties that came with the chemise were hardly clothing, more an eye patch in matching fabric, but she supposed they weren't intended for everyday wear.

Julian gripped the panties in his fist and tugged at them. They tore away without hesitation, and he tossed them onto the hotel room floor. Gretchen gasped in surprise, then started to giggle. There was a reason they were so flimsy. The giggles were abruptly stopped when the panties were replaced by Julian's hand.

Her back arched up off the couch, her hips both drawn to and shying from the powerful feelings his touch roused inside her. It was amazing just how quickly he could bring her to the edge. He'd learned her body's responses after only a few encounters.

Gretchen clenched her eyes shut, hovering on the

verge of release, when she felt cold air rush across her skin. Her eyes opened and she found that Julian had pulled back and was watching her as he lay against the far arm of the couch.

He slipped out of his briefs and beckoned her to join him. "Come here," Julian said.

Gretchen shook out of the robe, nervously took his hand and covered his body with her own. "What are we doing?"

"I'm not doing anything," he said with a sly smile. "I'm going to lie here and watch you while you take the lead."

Her jaw dropped in surprise. They'd moved on to an advanced class without warning. The idea of sitting astride Julian during sex while he watched her was incredibly unnerving. And arousing. She knew instantly that she wanted to do this. She could do this. She wouldn't let nerves get the best of her.

Julian reached for his toiletry case sitting on the coffee table and pulled out a condom. "Care to do the honors?"

She took it from him, determination setting in her jaw. Opening the package, she put it in place and slowly rolled it down the hard length of him. Julian let out a hiss as her hands worked up and down. His jaw was tight, his body tense. It was then that Gretchen realized she liked being in charge. This might be nerve-racking, but it was also going to be fun.

She rose up onto her knees, and Julian helped guide her movements as she lowered herself onto him. She moved slowly, painfully slow, as her body stretched to accommodate him. Then, at last, she found herself fully seated. Her core was already throbbing and prickling with the sensation of his previous touches. She couldn't imagine she would last long like this.

Biting her lip, she braced her hands on Julian's bare chest. She leaned forward and rocked back once, testing the waters. It was a delicious feeling, and judging by Julian's fingertips pressing fiercely into the flesh of her hips, she was doing something right.

Gretchen did it again, this time faster. Gaining confidence, she fell into a pleasurable rhythm with Julian muttering encouraging words to her.

His hands stroked the silk-and-lace fabric of her chemise as she moved, rising up to cover her breasts as they spilled over the top. She placed her hands over his and thrust her hips harder and faster against him.

"Julian," she whispered as she felt the release building up inside her.

"Yes, baby," he encouraged. "Just let go. Take me with you."

So she did. With renewed enthusiasm, she moved over him, opening the floodgates so that every ounce of pleasure, every emotion she held back, rushed free. In the moment, it wasn't his touch or her movements that sent her over the edge, it was the warm heat in the center of her chest.

She'd never felt this sensation before, but she knew what it was. Now that she and Julian had a future, she'd finally allowed herself to feel what she'd been fighting. Love. It was love that pushed her over the edge, crying out his name as the tremors of pleasure washed through her. As he followed suit, thrusting into her one last time, she looked down at him, placing her hand over his heart until they were both still and silent.

It was then that she collapsed against him. Gretchen

buried her face in his neck, breathing in the scent she'd become so used to so quickly.

This. The sex was nice, but *this* was what she'd truly waited twenty-nine years for.

Ten

Monday morning was a reality that neither of them really wanted to face. James's condition stabilized with the ventilator, and the doctors were extremely positive about his prognosis. He was moved out of the ICU, and his mother ushered Julian and Gretchen out the door and back to Nashville Sunday evening.

That night together had been a somber one, both of them knowing what Monday brought. Gretchen had to be in the office for her weekly staff meeting, so she slipped out of bed, leaving him a kiss as she ran out the door. She promised she would return after the meeting to say a proper goodbye before he had to leave for the airport.

They'd agreed they would give their relationship a real try, long distance be damned, but they both knew it would be hard. And different from how they'd spent the past few days. Julian worried about how they would pull it off. He had some time before his next film started shooting, but if he spent those weeks in Nashville, Ross would undoubtedly start complaining. He would want Julian in LA, doing readings, lining up his next part and being "seen." Unfortunately, he would probably want him being seen out on the town with a woman. That wasn't an option.

The only thing that got him up and dressed that morning was the knowledge that Ross was coming by to meet with him before he flew on to New York to arrange for a few press appearances. He'd much rather stay in bed and wait for Gretchen to return so he could make love to her one last time before he left.

He was drinking a protein shake he'd had stashed in his refrigerator when he heard his manager's knock on the door. Right on time, as usual. Julian opened the door, letting the short, squat man in the expensive suit into the room.

Ross wandered over to the sofa and sat down. "So, how'd the fake date go? The pictures I've seen looked pretty convincing, so good work. I know that couldn't have been easy to keep up."

Julian wasn't sure what his manager meant by that, but they should've been convincing. Every moment together was authentic and amazingly easy. "Actually, it was the easiest role I've played in years. After the first two days, I wasn't acting at all. In fact, Gretchen and I have really hit it off. I've asked her if I can continue to see her after this week."

The smug smile faded from Ross's face the longer Julian spoke. "Are you serious?"

Julian frowned at his manager. "I'm absolutely serious. She's a great woman. I've never dated anyone like her."

Ross sighed and ran his hand over his bald head. "I know that I set this up and I said that you dating a normal, everyday woman would be good for your image. But I never intended this to be a long-term arrangement."

"What does it matter if it's long-term or short-term? You wanted me to be with someone. I'm with someone. You should be happy."

"Not with her," Ross complained. "She's..."

Julian stared Ross down, daring him to insult Gretchen so he'd have a good reason to punch him. "She's *what*, Ross?"

Ross looked at him, preparing the words carefully. "She's not the kind of woman you'd want on your arm when you walk the red carpet at the Golden Globes. That's all I'm saying."

Julian snorted in contempt. "And when, in my illustrious career, have you ever booked me into a role that would get me invited to the Golden Globes?"

Ross shook his head. "You're missing the point. I'm sure she's a perfectly nice girl—the type you'd want to take home to meet your mother. But she's not the kind of girl that will take your career to the next level. Think Brad and Angelina. Tom and Nicole."

"Tom and Nicole are divorced."

"So it didn't work out," he said with a dismissive wave of his hand. "My point is that their high-profile marriage boosted their acting careers."

"There are plenty of famous actors and actresses with spouses that aren't in the business."

Ross leaned forward and rested his chin on his

pointed index fingers. "Julian, I'm your manager. You pay me to know what's best for your career. And I'm telling you—she is not the kind of woman Julian Cooper is supposed to be with."

If that was true, Julian wasn't certain if he wanted to be Julian Cooper anymore. His alter ego was becoming the kind of person he didn't even like. "You might be right, Ross, but I'm telling you that Gretchen is *exactly* the kind of woman that Julian *Curtis* wants to be with. This isn't a role, Ross, it's my life. I pay you to manage my career, but my private life is private. I'll date whomever I want to, and I'd appreciate it if you'd keep your mouth shut on the matter."

Ross's cell phone chimed and he looked down at the screen. Julian was happy for the interruption. The energy in the room had gotten far too tense. Ross was a good manager, but he needed to know he had boundaries.

Ross frowned at the phone and then let it down by his side. "You can date whomever you like, Julian, you're right. But you may want to reconsider choosing Gretchen."

"Why?"

"Did you tell her about James?"

Julian stiffened. "I had to. She was there when I got the call about him going into the hospital. But I told her she'd need to sign a confidentiality agreement."

"Did she?"

"Not yet. I was going to have you draw it up today."

Ross sighed and handed his phone over to him. "It's too damn late. The tragic story of Julian Cooper's secret twin has just hit the papers."

No. That wasn't possible. Julian scanned over the

article, looking for some kind of evidence that would prove that Ross was wrong. The sinking ache in his stomach didn't fade as he read the article. It was a huge, in-depth story about James, including his illness and recent hospital drama. Whoever had leaked the story had very up-to-date information about his brother.

"Who else knows about James?"

Julian shook his head. No one knew. "Just you and Murray. And Gretchen."

"Well, *I* certainly didn't leak the story."

He knew that was true, and with Murray on his honeymoon and worrying about anything but Julian and his brother, that left an unacceptable alternative. He just couldn't believe that Gretchen would sell him out and leak that story. She'd hardly seemed interested in the money he already owed her. But how much would the press be willing to pay for a story like this? Perhaps more than she could turn down?

"No," he insisted with a shake of his head. "I've been with her nonstop until this morning when she went to work. There's no way she could've contacted a reporter and sold that story without me knowing it."

Ross rolled his eyes. "Don't be so ignorant, Julian. You weren't with her every single second. You showered, you used the restroom, you slept. For all you know, she slipped out of bed in the night and emailed a reporter while you were satiated and unconscious."

Julian dropped into the chair beside him, the doubts finally creeping into his mind. He'd trusted her. Could Gretchen really have sold him out just like all the others?

A sad expression lined his manager's face as he reached out and patted Julian's shoulder. "I'm sorry, I really am. I know you think I'm a cold, heartless businessman, with all my confidentiality contracts and arranged relationships, but I've been in this business a long time. I've seen a lot of my clients get sold out by the people they trust the most. I try to protect my clients, but there's only so much I can do."

There was only one person who knew about everything that had happened with James over the past few days. The idea of that betrayal made his protein shake threaten to rise in the back of his throat. He didn't want to believe it. Every fiber in his being screamed that it couldn't be true. But Ross was right. There was no other answer.

"We've got to figure out how you want to handle this. Ignoring the article will make it seem like you're ashamed of your brother, which we don't want. It's probably best that we set up a tell-all interview of some kind, where you talk about him and explain why you tried to keep him out of the harsh spotlight."

"That sounds fine," Julian said in a flat tone. He really wasn't listening. At the moment, damage control was the last thing on his mind.

"While I'm handling that, you need to talk to Gretchen." He laid a fat envelope on the table. "Here's the money we owe her. Pay her and make her go away. Or I will."

Julian nodded. He knew Ross was right, but he didn't relish that conversation. "She's supposed to be coming over here today."

"When?"

Julian looked at the clock hanging on the hotel room wall. "Soon. She was coming back over before I left for the airport."

Ross nodded and stood up. "I'm going to head out, then. While I'm in New York, I'll see who I can talk to about that interview. When you get back to LA, call me and let me know how it went with Gretchen."

His manager slipped out of the room, but Julian hardly gave him any notice. The pain in his chest had subsided, leaving only the numbness of disassociation and the faint heat of anger licking at his ears. He knew what he had to do, and it was a role he didn't want to play. But play it he would to remove the malicious cancer from his life.

Gretchen had a hard time walking down the hallway to Julian's hotel room. A half hour ago, she'd damn near skipped down the same path, arriving earlier than she'd intended. She'd been so excited to see Julian one more time before he left that Natalie had let her cut out of the staff meeting early.

As she'd raised her hand to knock, she'd heard the sound of two men arguing loudly. She hadn't intended to listen in, but there was no way she was going to interrupt their argument. She'd decided to wait for a lull, then knock, but instead, she'd overheard more than she'd bargained for.

Ross's words haunted her, even now. *She is not the kind of woman Julian Cooper is supposed to be with,* he'd said. That hadn't surprised her. But when Julian said that he might be right, she'd felt her heart break. He'd done nothing over the past few days but tell her how beautiful she was, how worthy she was. To hear he really felt otherwise was a crushing blow to her fragile ego. She'd rushed to her car, sobbing against the steering wheel until she saw Ross leave.

She took a few minutes to recover from her tears and then headed back upstairs. She hadn't wanted to go back after that, but she knew it would be suspicious if she didn't show up. Taking a deep breath, she knocked on the door, more anxious than she'd been the very first day.

Julian was slow to answer, and when he did, she wished he hadn't. The light in his eyes was gone, his smile a distant memory. His jaw was tight in anger, his gaze burrowing into her as though he were searching her soul for some kind of guilt.

"Come in," he said, stepping back to let her inside.

This wasn't the reception she was hoping for, but she wasn't surprised. She sat down on the couch, clutching her purse in her lap. Without even speaking, she knew their relationship was about to unravel.

Julian picked up his phone from the coffee table and hit a few buttons. He wordlessly handed it to her, his blue eyes daring her to take it.

Gretchen hesitated, finally accepting the phone from him. When she looked down on the screen, she felt the air get sucked from her lungs. It was an article about James. She knew how hard Julian worked to maintain his brother's privacy, but now the secret was out. No wonder Julian was angry.

"How awful," Gretchen said, her hand coming up to cover her mouth. "How could anyone have found out about James? You were so careful. Could it have been one of the nurses at the hospital?"

"Good try," he said with a deadly cold tone. "I'm the actor in the room, not you."

Gretchen's gaze tore away from the phone to meet

his accusatory one. "What is that supposed to mean? Do you think I'm the one that leaked the story?"

Julian crossed his arms over his chest, looking larger and more intimidating than he ever had before. He looked as if he were about to mow down a field of terrorists with an automatic weapon, as in one of his films. "I don't have a lot of people to choose from, Gretchen. You're the only one who knows everything. You're the only one that's ever met my brother. No one else would have all these details."

Gretchen stood up. She was shorter than he was, but she couldn't just sit there and let him hover over her intimidatingly. "Just because I had the information doesn't mean I would've shared it. I told you that I wouldn't tell anyone about James and I meant it. I said I'd even sign your stupid agreement."

He nodded. "It never occurred to me that you'd manage to sell your story before I had time to draft the paperwork. A brilliant way to get around it, I have to say."

"Get around it?" she said, surprising herself with her own shrill tone. "I didn't get around anything, Julian, because I didn't sell this story. Did Ross feed you all these lies? I don't understand how you could think I'm capable of something like that."

"I didn't think you were capable of it, either." Despite his hard expression, Gretchen detected some hesitation in his eyes. He didn't seem to believe his own accusations, and yet he wouldn't back down.

"You're just using this as an excuse," she said, trying to bait the truth from him.

His brows went up in surprise. "An excuse for what?"

"To get rid of me," she accused. Ross's cruel words echoed in her head, fueling her own anger. "Despite all those promises you made in Louisville, you know I'm not the kind of woman that will boost your career."

Julian seemed baffled by her allegation. "What makes you say that?"

"I heard you talking to Ross," Gretchen said. "I got off work early and heard you arguing. I know I'm not the right kind of woman for Julian Cooper. I'm fat and I'm awkward. I don't have an elegant or graceful bone in my body. I know that. I don't need Ross or you or the press to point that out to me."

Julian shook his head angrily. "I don't know what you heard, but I can assure you that isn't what that discussion was about."

"It wasn't? Come on, Julian, be honest. As much as you claim you want to be this serious actor, you're hooked on that blockbuster lifestyle. You claim you can't quit because of your brother, but how much could his expenses possibly be? Are they as much as your Beverly Hills mansion? Your sports cars? Personal trainers and private chefs? Expensive baubles for your expensive women? I bet not. You're going to use this story to drop me because I don't fit into that lifestyle. I'm not going to help you become a bigger star."

"You know, this doesn't have anything to do with my lifestyle or my career. You obviously didn't hear the whole conversation with Ross or you wouldn't accuse me of such a thing. I would've happily walked the Gretchen I knew down any red carpet. I thought you were beautiful. Special. I meant every word I said to you, Gretchen. But that entire discussion I had with Ross is moot now, because I can't stand by and let you hurt my family."

Angry tears threatened to spill from Gretchen's eyes.

She didn't want to cry. Not in front of Julian, but the harder she fought it, the harder it became to hold the tears back. "I would never do that to you. Or to James. Or your mother. And if you think that I would, then you don't know me as well as you think you do."

"I guess not, but it's only been a few days, right? It's not like we were in love."

Gretchen flinched at how ridiculous he made the idea of love sound. She was grateful she had kept her budding feelings to herself. The last thing she needed was for him to throw that in her face.

"What did they offer you, Gretchen?" he taunted. His face was so twisted with anger and betrayal he didn't look anything like the Julian she knew. "Money? Was the ten grand I'm paying you not enough?"

"No, it isn't about the money. I don't care how much they would've offered me, I wouldn't have sold that story to the press. I don't even want the money from this week."

Julian rolled his eyes and picked up an envelope from the table. He thrust it into her hands and stepped away before she could reject the parcel. "Why don't you want the money? Don't need it after your big story payout?"

Gretchen was so upset, she didn't even look down at what he handed her. "There is no payout. There is no money. I don't know how to convince you of that. And I don't want your money because it feels wrong to take it when it felt like we were…more than just some fake Hollywood relationship."

His blue gaze tore away from hers, focusing on the beige carpet of the hotel room. "It was just acting, Gretchen. By making you think it was real, you were far more relaxed for the cameras. We never would've pulled this fake relationship off if you didn't think I really liked you."

That struck Gretchen dumb. Could he really mean that? Had he just played her because she was so stiff and awkward? She knew she wasn't good with men, but could she really be fooled that easily? He was an actor, after all, but she couldn't believe he'd misled her like that. He couldn't make eye contact when he said it. She was certain that there was more between them, but for some reason, he wouldn't let himself admit to the truth.

Her chin dropped to her chest, her gaze finally falling on the package in her hand. "What is this?" she asked.

"Ten thousand dollars, as agreed. You fulfilled your end of the bargain, and quite pleasurably at that." There was a gloating expression on his face that she didn't like. She'd been desperate to rid herself of her virginity, but she couldn't stand to have him gloat over taking it so easily.

"Obviously," he added bitterly, "the five-thousand-dollar bonus for keeping quiet about my brother was forfeited when you spilled your guts to that reporter."

Gretchen closed her eyes. She could feel her heart crumbling in her chest. There was no other explanation for the sharp sensation that stole her breath from her lungs. She had no words, but it didn't matter because she knew her words wouldn't make any difference. He'd decided she was guilty, and nothing would convince him otherwise.

And even if it did…what would it change? If he'd been pretending to like her just to get through the week, there was nothing between them to salvage. All she could do was hold it together long enough to get out of this hotel room with some of her dignity intact.

"Obviously," she said, steeling her nerves and matching his bitter tone.

When she opened her eyes, Julian was emerging from the bedroom with his rolling suitcase. Once again, he avoided her gaze, making a wide berth around her as he made his way to the door. "Enjoy Italy," he said. "I hope you can put that blood money to good use." Julian grabbed the handle of the door and flung it open, walking out of the hotel suite without so much as a backward glance.

Gretchen wanted to chase after him, to convince him that she was telling the truth, but her legs just wouldn't cooperate. She might not think much of herself, but she had too much pride to beg. Instead, her knees trembled and gave out, her body collapsing into the cushions of the couch. Her face dropped into her lap, this morning's second round of tears flowing freely and wetting the envelope in her hands.

She was a fool. A fool to believe that a man like Julian would ever want something to do with a woman like her. A fool to think that she could find happiness with a person so unobtainable. He was a fantasy.

And now, it had all come to an end.

Eleven

Gretchen had buried herself in work this week. It was easy with her job—there was always a wedding to decorate for, a consult with a couple, some design work to finish and send to the printers. Thank goodness. She needed the distraction.

Her two days off had been awful. She'd pretty much sat in her apartment crying and eating cookies. That wasn't going to help matters at all. But by the time she returned to the office, she had that out of her system. She was ready to focus on work and forget all about Julian Cooper.

Unfortunately, it wasn't that easy. Not with three nosy friends and coworkers who immediately noticed that the romantic bubble had burst. She'd left their staff meeting on Monday almost beaming and came back Thursday morning in mourning. She'd fought off the questions but gave them enough information to satisfy them: it was over. She didn't want to talk much more about it when it was so new. So far, they'd backed off, but only because they were busy preparing for the next wedding, too.

When the time came, she wasn't entirely sure what she would tell them. Getting up from her desk and going into her supply closet, she pulled down the bin labeled for this weekend's autumn-themed wedding. As she sorted through the paper products, she tried to work out the tale in her mind.

"He accused me of leaking a story to the press and we broke up," she said aloud. "And really, we were never actually together. He was just playing me." That sounded silly, especially out loud, despite every word being true.

Of course, the supposed truth was nothing compared to her secret worry. Would he really have used all that as an excuse to break up with her because when it came down to it, he needed to date a pretty actress, not a frumpy artist? He'd insisted that wasn't true. He'd done nothing but tell her how pretty she was while they were together, but was he just buttering her up for the part? She couldn't dismiss what she'd heard between him and Ross.

The worst part of it was that she had to admit that Ross was probably right. She wasn't what people expected. Vain, painted-up Bridgette made a lot more sense in their business, even if Julian didn't like it. As hard as he worked to keep his brother and family out of the spotlight, protecting Gretchen would be harder. While early press might be positive, eventually, she'd find herself on a cover with a headline that declared Julian demands she lose weight or it's over.

It would never work between them; she knew that now. It was a pipe dream, a fantasy that lasted only while he was playing the role of the adoring, doting boyfriend.

Her fingers went to her throat and sought out the opal necklace. She'd worn it nearly every moment since he bought it for her. She loved it. But it was time to take it off. She unlatched the clasp and let it pool in her hand. Looking down at the beautiful, ruined necklace, she opened her desk drawer and dropped it in with her pens and paper clips.

That done, Gretchen picked up the box of paper products and carried them out of her office. She quickly divided them up among the chapel, the entryway table and the ballroom.

The ballroom was still bare bones. This weekend's wedding was smaller and far less grand compared to Murray and Kelly's event, but there was still plenty to be done.

"Gretchen?"

Gretchen set down the programs and turned to find Natalie in the doorway behind her. "Hey."

"The linen delivery is here. Do you need help?"

She shrugged. "Sure, if you've got time."

Natalie nodded and they both went to the back to get the cleaned, pressed linens from the delivery truck. They rolled the cart back into the ballroom and Gretchen started laying them out on the tables. She could tell Natalie was lingering purposely, but she wasn't about to start the conversation she was dreading.

Her coworker joined her in laying out linens, this wedding using a chocolate brown with an ivory-and-gold lace overlay. After a minute, Natalie said in a quiet voice, "Are you okay?"

Gretchen sighed and finished spreading out the tablecloth. "No, but I'm getting there."

Natalie nodded. The wedding planner at From This Moment was the quiet, observant type. She did a lot of listening, both in her job and in her daily life, something most people didn't really do. By listening, she noticed a lot, most importantly what people weren't saying.

"How long do you think I have before Bree and Amelia will try to fix me up with someone else?" Gretchen had hoped that losing her virginity would take that pressure off her friends and their quest to get her a man, but she doubted that would be the case. With that sexual burden gone, they could just hunt down a normal guy for her, not some superhero worthy of her first time.

"I think you're safe through the holidays. It's too busy a time to try fixing someone up, although I wouldn't put it past Amelia to throw a Christmas party at her house and casually try introducing you to a couple single guys while you're there."

Gretchen could handle some awkward conversations at a party. That gave her a few weeks at least. She always liked Christmas, so having that distraction would keep her busy. She'd just have to be super careful about how many sugar cookies she consumed. She didn't need these twenty extra pounds turning into twenty-five.

"You could always take a page out of my book and go into holiday hibernation. Don't surface until the New Year's Eve hangovers fade away."

Gretchen had too much family for that, as nice as it might sound. Natalie was different; she had divorced parents and a general disdain for the holidays, so it was easier to fade away for a week or so. "Not everyone hates Christmas, Natalie. I can deal with the match-making as long as all the holiday festivities distract me."

"Maybe you should take some of that money and go on a little trip. You don't have enough time for Italy, but what about New York City or Vegas?"

Gretchen chuckled. "After what happened to Amelia in Vegas? No, thanks."

"I doubt you'll elope while you're there. But maybe you'll meet a hot distraction and spend some time catching up on all those vices you've missed out on."

Gretchen eased down into one of the chairs and shook her head. "I don't think I can spend any of that money. It feels…tainted somehow."

"What about Italy?"

"I'll get there someday. Just not any time soon. If I go now, all I'll see is old ruins and shells of what was. But if I wait long enough, maybe I can go with a man that loves me and I'll be able to see the beauty in it again. That would make the trip better, don't you think?"

Natalie smoothed out the fabric in front of her. "It sounds nice," she said with a noncommittal tone. Natalie was nearly as enthusiastic about love as she was about Christmas.

"If this last week taught me anything, it's that I'm worth more than I think. I just need the confidence to put myself out there and maybe I can have a healthy relationship with a normal guy."

"Absolutely," Natalie agreed. She came over and knelt beside Gretchen, giving her a comforting side hug. "You'll find someone if you want to. You can do anything you want to."

Gretchen had said the words, but she didn't entirely

believe them yet. Not even Natalie's assurances convinced her, but she would try. She wouldn't let her heart be trampled on by someone like Julian. She'd just reached too high, like Icarus, and crashed to the ground. If she'd opted to date someone safer, it might not have hurt as much to fall.

"Thanks, Natalie."

"I've got an appointment in a few minutes, but I'll try to check back and help you later."

Gretchen waved as Natalie slipped out of the ballroom. She watched her go and let her gaze drop into her lap. She would go to Italy someday, she knew that. But she wouldn't do it with the money Julian gave to her. He thought she was a sellout, and if she spent it, maybe she was.

Getting up, she went into her office and sat down at her desk. She opened the bottom drawer and pulled out her purse. Inside, she could see the thick wad of cash she'd stashed there in an envelope. She felt ridiculous walking around with ten grand in her bag, but it was all she could do until she made her decision.

Bree insisted that she go to Italy and drown her sorrows in a hot Italian lover. Amelia suggested that she mail it back to him if it bothered her to keep it and take her trip. While the idea of sipping prosecco in Capri as a sexy man who spoke very little English rubbed suntan lotion on her body seemed nice, she knew she couldn't do it. But sending it back would likely result in Julian rejecting the delivery, and she'd never get rid of the money.

That left a third option—to do something positive with the money, so no matter what, some good would come from the whole thing. If Gretchen did something worthwhile with the money, maybe it would purify it somehow. Make the past week have purpose. Julian might think she was a sneaky liar willing to sell him out, but nothing could be further from the truth. There was one way to make sure he knew it, too.

Logging on to her computer, she looked up the website for the Cerebral Palsy Foundation. With just a few clicks she found what she was looking for—a solution and a little peace of mind. All she had to do was deposit the money in her account and put the wheels in motion.

She might not get to go to Italy, but she would get the final word.

This script sucked. Julian could barely stand to continue reading the crap that Ross had couriered over this afternoon. It made *Bombs of Fury* look like Shakespeare.

A week ago, he would've accepted the offer without question, but that was before Gretchen had gotten under his skin. She'd planted those seeds of hope that he could have a serious acting career, then turned around and poured gasoline on the buds as they broke through the earth. Ross and his publicist were already scrambling to shift attention away from James and find a way to suppress the story without making it look as if Julian was embarrassed of his brother. He was anything but. He just didn't want press camped outside the Hawthorne Community or reporters pressing Julian for a sob story. He'd already gotten a call from Oprah to share his secret pain.

Despite Ross's assurances that it was the right path to take, Julian didn't want to share his secret pain. He wanted to keep his brother out of the spotlight, and he'd failed when he'd spilled his guts to Gretchen. He'd trusted her. Those big brown eyes had pleaded with him to confide in her. Then she'd turned around and stabbed him in the back just like all the others. He still couldn't quite believe it.

He tossed the offensive script onto the kitchen table and shook his head. He'd do it. He knew he would. But he'd loathe himself even more than he already did. Getting up from the table, he planned to march into the kitchen and make himself a stiff drink when he heard the sound of footsteps on the tile of the entryway.

No one was in the house but Julian. Before he could react, the intruder sauntered around the corner in a crop top and a pair of yoga pants. Bridgette.

"What the hell? How did you get in here?" Julian clenched his teeth at her bold move.

"I still have a key," she said, swinging her blond ponytail over her shoulder and smiling at him with a sweetness he didn't trust. She held up a bundle of letters in her hand and set them on the counter. "I brought in your mail. I came by because I heard you were back from the wedding and I wanted to see you."

She took a step toward him, but Julian stepped backward. He didn't like this. Bridgette was far too calculating to just pop in to be sociable. "Why?"

Bridgette pouted, her collagen-plumped bottom lip thrusting out. "Because I miss you, Julian. These last few weeks have been really hard on me."

"We broke up six months ago. Last I saw, you had your tongue down Paul's throat. You didn't seem like you were suffering to me."

She frowned, but the movement didn't translate to a furrowed brow because of all the Botox she injected.

"I was using Paul as a rebound. I was just trying to get over you, and it didn't work. When I saw those pictures of you and that fat girl, my heart nearly broke. I—"

"Stop," he interrupted, holding up his hand. Julian might be upset with Gretchen, but he wasn't going to let anyone else tear her down. He'd lied when he said she hadn't meant anything to him. It hadn't been acting, but it was the best thing to say. It convinced her, and him, that there was nothing to fight for. But despite all that, she still meant something to him. More than Bridgette ever had. "Gretchen is a beautiful, smart, sensitive woman that I cared about quite a bit. Be respectful of her or leave." He preferred she just leave, but he doubted he'd get rid of her that easily.

"Cared for her?" Bridgette whined. "You barely knew her. She must've worked hard to get her hooks into you that quickly. I could tell she was up to no good. I knew I had to find a way to get you back."

"You don't know what you're talking about. Gretchen didn't have hooks, much less ones in me. And even if she did, I don't need you to save me. If the choice were between the two of you, Gretchen would win." Even with the media leak and the lies, she was more genuine than Bridgette. In fact, that kind of thing was what he would've expected from his ex, which was why he'd never so much as breathed James's name in her presence.

"How could you still think that way about her after what she did? Selling the story about your brother to the press is just unforgivable."

Julian was about to argue with her when he stopped short. The article never mentioned the source for the story. Even if Bridgette had read the magazine from cover to cover, why would she presume that Gretchen had been the one to spill the news? How could she even know that Gretchen had knowledge of James to begin with? There was only one good reason for that.

"You did it." The sudden realization made his heart drop into his stomach with a nauseating thud.

Bridgette eyed him, a practiced look of vague innocence on her face. "I did what?" she asked with all the sweetness she could muster.

He didn't know how she'd dug up the truth, but he knew down to the depths of his soul that Bridgette had been the one to betray him. "You're the one that leaked the story about my brother."

"Me? How could I do that when I didn't know you had a brother? You never mentioned him or anything else about your family to me. I read about it in the gossip pages just like everyone else."

"No. You did this." Julian wasn't about to fall for her protests; they were far too polished. She was an actress, after all. "There's no way you could know that I'd blamed Gretchen for leaking the story unless you'd deliberately set it up to look that way. You got so jealous you did it deliberately to break up Gretchen and me. Admit it, or I'll track down the journalist and find out for myself. And if it was you, and you lied to me, every secret you've ever told me will be front-page news."

Bridgette's mouth dropped open, her eyes darting around the room in a panic. Nothing here was going to help her now, unless she was willing to bludgeon him with the ceramic jar on the countertop.

"I had to," she admitted at last. "It was the only way to get you away from Thunder Thighs. I had a detective following you in Nashville. I'd hired him just to keep tabs on you and get a feel for whether or not we had a chance to reconcile. Then he tailed you to Louisville and uncovered the truth about your brother. I wouldn't have said a word about it, but then I realized that you took her with you. You'd never said a word about James to me in over a year together and yet you took *her* to meet him. I was devastated, Julian. I didn't know what to do. I thought if the story leaked, you'd blame her and come home so distraught I could comfort you and we'd get back together."

Bridgette was crazier than even he gave her credit for. "You plan is flawed, Bridgette. I did blame her and I did come home distraught, but I don't want you to comfort me. I want you to go away."

"Please, Julian. We could be a Hollywood power couple. Admit it, we just make sense together. A heck of a lot more sense than you and the pudgy artist."

"Get out!" he roared, his anger turning on like the flick of a switch. He wasn't going to have her in his presence insulting the woman he loved for one more minute.

"Julian, I—"

Julian lunged forward and snatched his house keys out of her hand. He wouldn't make that mistake twice. "Get out before I call the cops *and* the press so they can photograph you getting arrested for trespassing."

Her eyes widened. He could tell she was trying to figure if he was bluffing or not. After a moment, she decided not to press her luck. Flinging her hair defiantly over her shoulder, she spun on her heel and marched down the hallway, proudly displaying the word JUICY in big letters across her rear end. Julian watched as she opened the front door and looked back at him. "You'll regret losing me one day, Julian."

Instead of responding, he waved his fingers in a happy dismissal. She stormed out, slamming the door shut behind her. Julian followed her path down the hallway, flipping the dead bolt and arming the perimeter alarm system in case she tried to sneak back in and boil a rabbit or something.

With a heavy sigh of relief, he traveled back to the kitchen. He tossed the keys down by the stack of mail and started sorting through the letters that Bridgette had no doubt snooped through before bringing them inside. The last letter in the stack had the logo of the Cerebral Palsy Foundation on the front.

Setting the rest aside, he opened the envelope. It was a letter informing him that an anonymous donation had been made to the foundation in his and James's names. That brought a smile to his face. Perhaps having James's story hit the news wasn't bad after all. Now that it was done, perhaps being vocal about it would bring some much-needed attention to the cause. The foundation had even featured a story about them on the site with the link to donate to the cause in their name. If someone had seen the story and made a donation because of it, perhaps it was worth the angst that came along with it.

Turning to the next page, he saw that the amount donated was ten thousand dollars. That was no paltry donation. His eyes remained glued to the number, a nagging feeling prickling at the back of his neck.

Ten thousand dollars. That was exactly how much he'd left in cash for Gretchen when he'd stormed out. She'd said she didn't want his money, but he'd forced it on her. Was this her way of giving the money back and proving she was the bigger person at the same time?

Julian suddenly felt weak in the knees. He wasn't

used to experiencing that feeling outside of the gym. He slumped down onto a stool at the kitchen counter and looked over the letter again. The timing was far too perfect for it to be from anyone else.

He was a jerk. He knew that now. The only reason she'd gotten involved in this whole mess was because she'd wanted to take that money and go to Italy. All the drama and the heartache were for nothing. She'd handed the money away along with her dream.

Julian dropped the letter onto the counter and squeezed his eyes shut. Gretchen was the only person in his life who didn't want or need anything from him but his love and his trust. Without realizing the depths of his feelings for her, he'd given her both, then snatched them away, accusing her of terrible things and throwing cash at her as he left as though she were a common whore.

Picking up his phone, he dialed his travel agent. He didn't stop to think or worry about what Ross would say. He didn't care. All Julian knew was that he needed to get back to Nashville as soon as possible.

Once his arrangements were made, he started to formulate the rest of his plan. There were several hours before his flight, and he needed to make some important stops on the way to LAX.

He just prayed it wasn't too late to make this right.

Twelve

The red-eye from Los Angeles landed Julian back in Nashville around sunrise on Saturday morning. He grabbed his rental car and tore off in the direction of the chapel.

He was expecting the place to be mostly empty given that it was just past 7:00 a.m., but the lot was filled with vans and trucks with vendor logos on the side. Wedding preparation apparently started early. Among them was Gretchen's green sedan.

Parking his rental out of the path of the big trucks, he followed a man with a giant vase of deep red, orange and yellow flowers through the back door and over to the ballroom.

The room was bustling with people. There were men on lifts adjusting the lighting in the rafters, at least half a dozen people handling flowers, an orchestra setting up on stage, and a few people setting out glassware and other table decor. In the middle of all the chaos was Gretchen. Despite everything going on around them, his eyes went to her in an instant.

Her hair was curly today. He'd gotten used to her straightening it while the cameras were around, but now that their farce of a relationship was over, she'd let it just be curly again. Julian liked it curly. The other style was chic and fashionable, but the wild curls were more suited to the free artist he saw in Gretchen.

She had on a pair of dark denim skinny jeans with ballet flats and a sweater in a rusty color that seemed to go with the fall decor of the day's event. Her back was to him when he came in. She was busily directing some activity in the corner where Murray and Kelly had placed their wedding cake.

With determination pumping through his veins and pushing him forward, he meandered through the maze of tables and chairs to the far corner of the room. No one paid any attention to him. He was only ten or so feet away when Gretchen finally turned around. As her eyes met his, she froze in place, clutching her tablet to her chest as though it was the only thing holding her on the Earth.

Julian smiled, hoping that would help soften the shock, but it didn't. She did recover, but it only resulted in a frown lining her brow and tightening her jaw. He wouldn't let that deter him, though. She was angry. She had a right to be angry after he turned on her like that. He'd expected this response when he got on the plane. But he would convince her that he was sorry and things would be okay. He was certain of it.

"What are you doing here, Julian?" Her voice was

flat and disinterested, matching the expression on her face. The only thing that gave her away was the slight twinkle in her dark eyes. Was it interest? Irritation? Attraction? Perhaps it was just an overhead pin light giving him hope where there was none to be had.

"I came back to talk to you," he said, taking a step toward her and hoping for the best.

Gretchen didn't retreat, but her posture didn't welcome him closer, either. "I think we've done plenty of talking, don't you agree?"

"Not about this." He took another step forward. "Gretchen, I'm so sorry about Monday. The whole situation with Ross, the news article... I know now that none of that had to do with you, and I'm sorry for blaming you for it. You were right when you said you would never do anything like that to me. And I knew it. But I've had so many people betray my trust in the past. Someone had to be to blame, and I didn't know who else could possibly be involved."

She nodded, setting down her tablet so she could cross her arms over her chest. "Jumping to unfounded conclusions tends to cause problems. I'm glad you found the real culprit. I hope you made them suffer the way you made me suffer the last few days. It seems only fair."

Julian watched a flicker of pain dance across her face, and he hated that he was the one to cause it. He had to fix this. "It was Bridgette," he admitted. "She had a detective following me around Nashville and up to Louisville. He dug up the whole story, and then she leaked it because she was jealous of you and wanted to break us up."

Gretchen snorted at his words. "Bridgette Martin...

is jealous…of *me*? How is that even possible? She's one of the most beautiful women I've ever seen."

"Like I told you before, Gretchen, it's all an illusion. I work in a business where everyone tries to tear you down. Even someone like Bridgette isn't immune to scathing critique, and their ego can be fragile because of it. You were a threat to her. She's a woman used to getting what she wants, and she was going to get me back by any means necessary."

"Those silicone implants must have leached chemicals into her brain."

Julian smiled. "Perhaps. But I wanted you to know that it didn't work. Even before I knew the truth about what she'd done, I didn't want her. I still wanted you."

Her dark gaze narrowed at him. "No, you don't," she said with certainty in her voice.

"I do," he insisted. "I did then and I still do. Even when I was angry at you, I only pushed you away because I knew I had to or risk another story in the papers. I didn't want to let you go, though. These days without you have felt so empty, like I've just been going through the motions. I miss having you in my life."

He expected Gretchen to echo his words, to say that she missed him, too, but she stayed silent.

"And then, just when I didn't think I could feel like a bigger jerk, I got the letter from the Cerebral Palsy Foundation. When I saw it, I knew the donation had come from you."

"How do you know it was from me? It was anonymous."

Julian shook his head. "It was, but it had you written all over it. I made you take the money when you didn't want it, so you returned it in a way that even I couldn't argue with. It was brilliant, really, but it just confirmed in my mind that I had been right about you all along."

Her brow went up slightly. "Right about what?"

"Right when I thought that you were one of the sweetest, most giving creatures I'd ever met. That you didn't want anything from me but my love, unlike so many others in my life. You could've taken that money and blown it and forgotten all about me. But you didn't. You couldn't return it, so you used it in the best possible way. A way that could help my brother."

"I hope it does," she said. "Something good should come of the last week's chaos."

Julian's chest clenched at her words. Did she really think what they had was nothing more than a muddled mess? "It might have been chaotic, but I loved every minute of it." Julian hesitated and took a deep breath before he said the words he'd been waiting to say. "And I love you, Gretchen."

Her eyes widened at his declaration, but the response stopped there. No smile, no blush, no rushing into his arms. She certainly didn't respond in kind, as he'd hoped. She just stood there, watching him in her suspicious way.

"I mean it," he continued in a desperate need to fill the silence. "You've changed me in such a profound way that even if you throw me out of here and never speak to me again, there's no way I can go back to living life the way I had before. I've told Ross that I want to take the role in that independent film we discussed. They're going to be filming in Knoxville, Tennessee, in the summer. I've got some re-shoots between now and Christmas, and then another shoot-'em-up movie to film this spring, but after that I'll be out this way for months."

Gretchen swallowed hard, her throat working before she spoke. "You'll like Knoxville," she replied casually.

"What I'll like is being closer to you."

"For a few months. And then what?" she pressed.

"And then I move to Nashville."

That got her attention. This time it was Gretchen who took a step forward, stopping herself before she got too close. "What are you going to do here?"

Julian shrugged. He didn't have all that worked out yet, but he knew that he wanted his home base to be here with Gretchen, even if he had to travel to the occasional movie set or publicity event. "Whatever I want to do. Theater. Television. Smaller-budget films. I could even teach. You were right when you said I was using my brother as an excuse. I have plenty of money to care for him. Even if I just invested the income from *Bombs of Fury* and never acted again, I could probably keep him comfortable for the rest of his life. The truth is that I was scared to try something new. Afraid to fail."

Gretchen's expression softened as she looked at him. "You're not going to fail, Julian."

"Thank you. You believe in me even when I have a hard time believing in myself. You give me the strength I didn't know I was missing. Having you there by my side when we visited James...you have no idea how much that meant to me. I need you in my life, Gretchen. I love you."

He reached into his pocket and grasped the ring he'd hidden there. As he pulled it out, he closed his eyes and sank to one knee, praying that his words had been sincere enough to quell her doubts so she could accept his proposal.

He opened the lid on its hinge, exposing the ring he'd

selected specially for her. The large oval diamond was set in delicate rose gold with a halo of micro-diamonds encircling it and wrapping around the band. The moment he saw it, he knew the ring was perfect for her. "Gretchen, will you—?"

"No!" she interrupted, stealing the proposal from his lips.

Julian looked startled at her sudden declaration, but Gretchen was even more surprised. The word had leaped from her mouth before she could stop it.

His mouth hung agape for a moment, and then he recovered. "The jeweler recommended this cut for a woman who was artistic and daring. I thought that suited you perfectly. Do you not like it? We can get a different one. You can pick whatever you want."

Of course she liked it. She loved it. It was beautiful and sparkly and perfect and she wanted to say yes. But how could she? "It isn't about the ring, Julian."

"Wow. Okay." He snapped the ring box shut and stood up. He glanced around the room nervously, as though he hoped none of the suppliers had witnessed his rebuff. Thankfully everyone was too busy to notice them in the corner.

"Julian." She reached out to touch his arm. "We need to talk about this."

His jaw flexed as he clenched his teeth. "It sounds like you've said all you needed to say. You don't want to marry me. That's fine."

"I never said that."

His blue eyes searched her face in confusion. "I proposed and you said no. Quite forcefully, actually."

Gretchen sighed. She'd botched this. "I wasn't saying no to the proposal. I wanted you to stop for a minute so I could say something first."

The lines in his forehead faded, but he didn't seem convinced that she wasn't about to drop him like a rock. "What do you want to say?"

"I care about you, Julian. I'm in love with you. But I'm not sure if that's enough to sustain a marriage. How can I know that you love me? Truly? How does either of us know that you don't just like the way I make you feel? Yes, I support you. I care about you and make you feel ten feet tall when everyone else is trying to tear you down or get something from you. Are you proposing to that feeling you get when you're with me, or are you actually proposing to me?"

"I'm proposing to you. Of course I am." He seemed insulted by her question, but it couldn't be helped. She needed to know before she fully invested not only her heart, but her life in this relationship.

"That all sounds wonderful. This whole speech of yours has been riveting. Award-caliber material. I think you'll do great in that independent film. But standing here, right now, how can I know that you mean what you say and that it's not some over-rehearsed script? You said that I wasn't the kind of woman Julian Cooper should be with. I heard you agree with Ross when you thought I wasn't listening. For you to turn around and propose not long after…it doesn't leave me feeling very confident about us. Are you going to drop me when the next hot young thing hits the scene and Ross pushes her at you?"

Julian closed his eyes a moment and nodded. "I did say that to Ross. You're not the kind of woman international action star Julian Cooper should be with. But if you'd stayed one moment longer, you would've heard me say that you're the perfect woman for Julian Curtis. And that Julian Curtis wasn't interested in his manager's opinion of his personal life."

Gretchen gasped. She didn't even know what to say to that. Could he really mean it?

"Gretchen," Julian said, moving close to her and placing his reassuring palms on her upper arms. "This isn't a rehearsed script. This isn't Julian Cooper standing in front of you right now reciting lines. This is Julian Curtis, a guy from Kentucky," he said with his accent suddenly coming through, "telling you how he truly feels and asking you to marry him. Do you believe me?"

Her head was spinning. With Julian so close, the warm scent of him was filling her lungs and his touch was heating her skin through her sweater. She could resist him from a distance, but when he stood there, saying all the right words the way he was now, she had no defenses. All she could do was nod.

Julian smiled and slipped back onto one knee. "Now, I'm going to try this again and I want you to let me finish before you answer, okay?"

Gretchen nodded again as Julian pulled out the ring box and opened it a second time. He took her hand in his and looked up at her with his soulful blue eyes.

"I love you, Gretchen, with all my heart. I know there are going to be people out there that think you're so lucky—a regular woman from Tennessee landing a big movie star—but they're wrong. If you accept my proposal and agree to marry me, I can assure you that I'm the lucky one. Every morning I wake up with you beside me is a day I count my lucky stars that you're in my life and have chosen me as the man you love.

Gretchen McAlister, would you do me the great honor of being Mrs. Julian Curtis?"

Gretchen waited half a heartbeat to answer. Not because she didn't want to say yes, but because she wanted to make sure she didn't interrupt him this time. When she was certain he was finished, she said "Yes!" with a broad smile spreading across her face.

Julian slipped the ring onto her finger, the tears in her eyes blurring her view of the sparkly jewelry. It didn't matter. She had a lifetime to look at it. Once he stood up, Gretchen launched herself into his arms. She wrapped her arms around his neck and pulled him close. There, with her nose buried in the hollow of his throat, she finally got to return to a place she thought she might never visit again.

Julian hugged her fiercely and then tipped her head up so that he could press his lips to hers. The kiss was gentler, sweeter, more wonderful than she could've expected.

What an emotional roller coaster the past week had been. She'd gone from the top of the world to the pits of despair and back in only a few days' time. Gretchen was no expert on this love business, but she hoped that it would level out. Her heart couldn't take the drama. But she could take fifty or sixty more years in his strong arms.

"We need to go to Italy," Julian proclaimed, drawing Gretchen from her spinning thoughts.

"Right now?"

Julian smiled and shook his head. "No, not right now. Unless you want to hop on a plane and elope... It might be the only way we can manage to get married without the press finding out."

Elope? She wasn't so sure about that. Amelia had not recommended her quickie Vegas wedding to others. "I'd rather not elope," she said, "but if you want to get married in Italy, that sounds amazing."

"That's what we'll do, then. You gave away your chance to go to Italy when you donated all that money, so it only seems right that we go there to get married, or at the very least, for the honeymoon."

Gretchen could just envision it in her mind. "A tiny rustic chapel in Tuscany. Or maybe a winery on a hill overlooking the poppies and sunflowers."

Julian tightened his grip on her waist. "Anything you want. You're marrying a movie star, after all. There's no cutting corners for an event like this. I can even call George to see if we can have it at his place on Lake Como if you want."

George? She blinked and shook her head. She would be perfectly comfortable as Mrs. Julian Curtis, but it would take a while for her to get used to the idea of their public lives as Mr. and Mrs. Julian Cooper, friends of movie stars, musicians and other famous people.

"That's probably a little more over-the-top than I was thinking," she admitted. Marrying Julian was enough of a fantasy come true. Having the wedding in Italy was more than she could ever ask for. She wanted to keep it simple, though. She didn't want to burn through a fortune on the first day of their marriage. They had a long life together ahead of them, and she wanted to celebrate every day, not just the first. "I just want something small with all our family, some amazing food and wine and scenery that can't be beat by any decoration you could buy."

"I think I can handle that. I'll add that I want to see

you in a beautiful gown that showcases all those luscious curves. I want flickering candles all over to make your skin glow like flawless ivory. And after we eat all that amazing food, I want to dance with you under the stars. This spring, I'll have a month off between filming. How does May sound to you? We can get married and then spend a few weeks exploring every nook and cranny Italy has to offer."

"Perfect," she said, and she meant it. She couldn't imagine a wedding or a husband any more wonderful.

A sound caught her attention. Looking around Julian's broad shoulders, Gretchen noticed three women hovering in the doorway of the ballroom, not working like the others. A blonde, a redhead and a brunette. Even from this distance she could hear the high twitter of their fevered discussion of Julian's return. He'd probably slipped in the back door, but it didn't matter. You couldn't get anything past those three. She also knew that they wouldn't go away until she told them what they wanted to know.

Raising her left hand in the air, she flashed the sparkling diamond at them and wiggled her fingers. It was a large enough setting that even from across the ballroom, the gesture was easily decipherable. A whoop and a few squeals sounded from the entrance.

Gretchen turned away to look up at her fiancé and smiled. "Block a week off the calendar next spring, ladies," she shouted while she focused only on him. "We're all going to Italy for a wedding!"

Epilogue

"Christmas is coming."

Gretchen's brow went up at Natalie's morose declaration. "You sound like a character in *Game of Thrones*. Of course Christmas is coming. It's almost December, honey, and it's one of the more predictable holidays."

Her friend set down her tablet and frowned. Gretchen knew that Natalie didn't like Christmas. She'd never pressed her friend about why she despised the beloved holiday, but she knew it was true and had been since back when they were in college. Every year, the chapel would shut down for the week or so between Christmas Eve and New Year's Day. Natalie claimed it was a built-in vacation for everyone, but Gretchen wondered if there wasn't more to it.

Natalie was a workaholic to begin with, but when December rolled around, she redoubled her efforts. She claimed that she wanted to get a head start on the accounting and taxes for the end of the year, but Gretchen was certain that she was trying to avoid anything to do with Christmas.

While Bree might stroll into the office wearing reindeer antlers that lit up and Amelia might try to organize a holiday party, Natalie did not participate. She insisted they not exchange gifts, arguing they were just passing money around and it was pointless.

Natalie wasn't a Grinch, per se. She wasn't out to stop everyone from having a good holiday. She just didn't want others to subject her to their merriment. That usually meant she hid in her house and didn't leave for a solid week, or she went on a trip somewhere.

Even then, she couldn't avoid everything. Always the professional, Natalie usually had to coordinate a couple winter- or holiday-themed weddings this time of year. There was no avoiding it. Especially when one of this year's weddings was the wedding of Natalie's childhood best friend, Lily.

Natalie leaned back in her office chair and ripped the headset off, tossing it onto her desk. "It's bothering me more than usual this year."

"Are you taking a trip or staying home?" Gretchen asked.

"I'm staying home. I was considering a trip to Buenos Aires, but I don't have time. We squeezed Lily's last-minute wedding in on the Saturday before Christmas, so I'll be involved in that and not able to do the normal end-of-year paperwork until it's over."

"You're not planning to work over the shutdown, are you?" Gretchen planted her hands on her hips. "You don't have to celebrate, but by damn, you've got to take the time off, Natalie. You work seven days a week sometimes."

Natalie dismissed her concerns. "I don't work the late hours you and Amelia do. I'm never here until midnight."

"It doesn't matter. You're still putting in too much time. You need to get away from all of this. Maybe go to a tropical island and have some kind of a fling with a sexy stranger."

At that, Natalie snorted. "I'm sorry, but a man is not the answer to my problems. That actually makes it worse."

"I'm not saying fall in love and marry the guy. I'm just saying to keep him locked in your hotel suite until the last New Year's firecracker explodes. What can a night or two of hot sex hurt?"

Natalie looked up at Gretchen with her brow furrowed painfully tight. "It can hurt plenty when the guy you throw yourself at is your best friend's brother and he turns you down flat."

* * * * *

Pick up these other BRIDES AND BELLES
stories from Andrea Laurence:
Wedding planning is their business...and
their pleasure.

SNOWED IN WITH HER EX
THIRTY DAYS TO WIN HIS WIFE

Available now!

A WHITE WEDDING CHRISTMAS
Available December 2015

Only from Harlequin Desire!

If you're on Twitter, tell us what you think
of Harlequin Desire! #harlequindesire

RECLAIMED BY
THE RANCHER
Janice Maynard

One

Not much rattled Jeff Hartley. At twenty-nine, he owned and operated the family ranch where he had grown up during a near-idyllic childhood. His parents had taken early retirement back in the spring and had headed off to a condo on Galveston Bay, leaving their only son to carry on the tradition.

Jeff was a full member of the prestigious Texas Cattleman's Club, a venerable establishment where the movers and shakers of Royal, Texas, met to shoot the breeze and oftentimes conduct business. Jeff prided himself on being mature, efficient, easygoing and practical.

But when he opened his door on a warm October afternoon and saw Lucy Peyton standing on his front porch, it felt as if a bull had kicked him in the chest. First there was the dearth of oxygen, a damned scary feeling. Then the pain set in. After that, he had the impulse to flee before the bull could take another shot.

He stared at his visitor, his gaze as level and dispassionate as he could make it. "I plan to vote Democrat this year. I don't need any magazine subscriptions. And I already have a church home," he said. "But thanks for stopping by."

He almost had the door closed before she spoke. "Jeff. Please. I need to talk to you."

Damn it. How could a woman say his name—one measly syllable—and make his insides go all wonky? Her voice was every bit the same as he remembered. Soft and husky...as if she were on the verge of laryngitis. Or perhaps about to offer some lucky man naughty, unspeakable pleasure in the bedroom.

The sound of eight words, no matter how urgently spoken, shouldn't have made him weak in the knees.

Her looks hadn't changed, either, though she was a bit thinner than he remembered. Her dark brown hair, all one length but parted on the side, brushed her shoulders. Hazel eyes still reminded him of an autumn pond filled with fallen leaves.

She was tall, at least five-eight...and though she was athletic and graceful, she had plenty of curves to add interest to the map. Some of those curves still kept him awake on dark, troubled nights.

"Unless you're here to apologize," he said, his words deliberately curt, "I don't think we have anything to talk about."

When she shoved her shoulder against the door, he had to step back or risk hurting her. Even so, he planted himself in the doorway, drawing a metaphorical line in the sand.

Her eyes widened, even as they flashed with temper. "How *dare* you try to play the wronged party, you *lying, cheating, sonofa*—"

Either she ran out of adjectives, or she suddenly realized that insulting a man was no way to gain entry into his home.

He lifted an eyebrow. "You were saying?"

His mild tone seemed to enrage her further, though to her credit, she managed to swallow whatever additional words trembled on her tongue. Was it bad of him to remember that small pink tongue wetting his— Oh, hell. Now *he* was the one who pulled up short. Nothing stood to be gained by indulging in a sentimental stroll down memory lane.

No tongues. No nothing.

She licked her lips and took a deep, visible breath. "Samson Oil is trying to buy the Peyton ranch."

Two

Lucy was diabetic; she'd been diagnosed as a twelve-year-old. If she didn't take her insulin, she sometimes got the shakes. But nothing like this. Facing the man she had come to see made her tremble from head to toe. And she couldn't seem to stop. No amount of medicine in the world was ever going to cure her fascination with the ornery, immoral, two-faced, spectacularly handsome Jeff Hartley.

At the moment, however, he was her only hope.

"May I come in?" she asked, trying not to notice the way he smelled of leather and lime and warm male skin.

Jeff stared at her long enough to make her think he might actually say no. In the end, however, gentlemanly manners won out. "Ten minutes," he said gruffly. "I have plans later."

If he meant to wound her, his barb was successful...

though she would never give him the satisfaction of knowing for sure. As they navigated the few steps into his living room and sat down, she found herself swamped with memories. This old farmhouse dated back three generations. It had been lovingly cared for and well preserved.

For one brief second, everything came crashing back: the hours she had spent in this bright, cheerful home, the master bedroom upstairs with the queen-size mattress and double-wedding-ring quilt, the bed Jeff had complained was too small for his six-foot-two frame...

She didn't want to remember. Not at all. Not even the spot in this very room where Jeff Hartley had gone down on one knee and offered her a ring and his heart.

Dredging up reserves of audacity and courage, she ignored the past and cut to the chase. "My cousin is trying to sell his land to Samson Oil." Recently, the outsider company had begun buying up acreage in Royal, Texas, at an alarming rate.

Jeff sat back in a leather armchair and hitched one ankle across the opposite knee, drawing attention to his feet. "Is it a fair offer?"

Nobody Lucy had ever known wore scuffed, hand-tooled cowboy boots as well as Jeff Hartley. At one time she wondered if he slept in the damned things. But then came that memorable evening when he showed her how a woman could take off a man's boots at the end of the day...

Her face heated. She jerked her thoughts back to the present. "More than fair. But that's not the point. The property has been in the Peyton family for almost a century. The farmland has contributed to Maverick County's food supply for decades. Equally important—the wildlife preserve was my grandfather's baby. Samson Oil will ruin everything."

"Why does Kenny want to sell?"

"He's sick of farming. He swears there's nothing for him in Royal anymore. He's decided to move to LA and try for an acting career. He pointed out that I sold most of my share to him, left for college and then stayed away. He wants his chance. But he needs cash."

"And this is my problem, how?"

Three

Lucy bit her lip until she tasted blood in her mouth. She couldn't afford to let Jeff goad her into losing her temper. It had happened far too easily on his front porch a moment ago. Her only focus right now should be on getting what she needed to stop a bad, bad decision.

It might have helped if Jeff had gotten old and fat in the past two years. But unfortunately, he looked better than ever. Dark blond hair in need of a trim. Piercing green eyes, definitely on the hostile side. And a long, lean body and lazy gait that made grown women sigh with delight whenever he sauntered by.

"I need you to loan me twenty thousand dollars," she blurted out. "The farm is self-supporting, but Kenny doesn't have a lot of liquid assets. He may be bluffing. Even if he's serious, though, twenty grand will get him off my back and send him on his way. He thinks the only choice he has for coming up with relocation funds is to unload the farm, but I'm trying to give him another option."

"What will happen to the farm when he goes to the West Coast?"

It was a good question. And one she had wrestled with ever since Kenny told her he wanted to leave town. "I suppose I'll have to come back to Royal and take over. At least until Kenny crashes and burns in California and decides to return home."

"You don't have much faith in him, do you?"

She shrugged. "Our fathers were brothers. So we share DNA. But Kenny has always had a problem with focus. Six months ago he wanted to go to vet school. Six months before that he was studying to take the LSAT."

"But you already have a career…right? As a physical trainer? In Austin? That fancy master's degree you earned in sports medicine won't do you much good out on the farm." He didn't even bother to hide the sarcasm.

She wanted to squirm, but she concentrated on breathing in and breathing out, relaxing her muscles one set at a time. "Fortunately, mine is the kind of job that's in demand. I'm sure they won't hold my exact position, but there will be plenty of similar spots when I go back."

"How long do you think you'll have to stay here in Royal?"

"A few months. A year at the most. Will you loan me the money, or not?"

Jeff scowled. "You've got a lot of balls coming to me for help, Lucy."

"You *owe* me," she said firmly. "And you know it."

This man…this beautiful, rugged snake of a man had been responsible for the second worst day of her life.

He sat up and leaned forward, resting his elbows on his knees. His veneer of calm peeled away, leaving a male who was a little bit frightening. Dark emerald eyes judged her and found her wanting. "I don't *owe* you a single damn thing. You're the one who walked out on our wedding and made me a laughingstock in Royal."

She jumped to her feet, heart pounding. Lord, he made her mad. "Because I caught you at our rehearsal dinner kissing the maid of honor," she yelled.

Four

Something about Lucy's meltdown actually made Jeff feel a little bit better about this confrontation. At least she wasn't indifferent.

"Sit down, Lucy," he said firmly. "If money is going to change hands, I have two conditions."

She did sit, but the motion looked involuntary...as if her knees gave out. "Conditions?"

"It's a lot of money. And besides, why ask me? Me, of all people?"

"You're rich," she said bluntly, her stormy gaze daring him to disagree.

It was true. His bank account was healthy. And sadly, Lucy had no family to turn to, other than her cousin. Lucy's parents and Kenny's had been killed in a boating accident eight years ago. Because of that tragedy, Lucy had a closer relationship with her cousin than one might expect. They were more like siblings, really.

"If my bottom line is good, it's partly because I don't toss money out the window on a whim."

"It wouldn't be a whim, Jeff. I know the way you think. This thing with Samson Oil is surely eating away at you. *Outsiders*. Taking over land that represents the history of Royal. And then doing God knows what with it. Drilling for oil that isn't there. Selling off the dud acres. Shopping malls. Big box stores. Admit it. The thought makes you shudder. You have to be suspicious about why a mysterious oil company is suddenly trying to buy land that was checked for oil years ago."

That was the problem with old girlfriends. They knew a man's weaknesses. "You're not wrong," he said slowly, taken aback that she had pegged him so well. "But in that case, why wouldn't I buy Kenny's land outright? And make sure that it retains its original purpose?"

"Because it's not the honorable thing to do. Kenny will see the light one day soon. And he would be devastated to come back to Royal and have nothing. Besides, that would be a whole lot more money. Twenty thousand is chicken feed to you."

Jeff grimaced. "You must know some damn fine chickens."

Perhaps she understood him better than he wanted to admit, because after laying out her case, she sat quietly, giving him time to sort through the possibilities. Lucy stared at him with hazel eyes that reflected wariness and a hint of grief.

He felt the grief, too. Had wallowed in it for weeks. But a man had to move on with his life. At one time, he'd been absolutely sure he would grow old with this woman. Now he could barely look at her.

"I need to think about it," he said.

Lucy's temper fired again. "Since when do you have trouble making decisions?" Her hands twisted together in her lap as if she wanted to wrap them around his neck.

"Don't push me, Lucy." He scowled at her. "I'll pick you up out at the farm at five. We'll have dinner, and I'll give you my answer."

Her throat worked. "I don't want to be seen with you."

Five

The barb wasn't unexpected, but it took Jeff's breath momentarily. "The feeling is mutual," he growled. "I'll make reservations in Midland. We'll discuss my terms."

"But that's fifty miles away."

Her visible dismay gave him deep masculine satisfaction. It was time for some payback. Lucy deserved to twist in the wind for what she had done to him. A man's pride was everything.

"Take it or leave it," he said, the words curt.

"I thought you had plans later."

"You let me worry about my calendar, sweetheart."

He watched her flinch at his overt sarcasm. For a moment, he was ashamed of baiting her. But he shored up his anger. Lucy deserved his antagonism and more.

The silence grew in length and breadth, thick with unspoken emotions. If he listened hard enough, he thought he might even be able to hear the rapid beat of her heart. Like a defenseless animal trapped in a cage of its own making.

"Lucy?" He lifted an eyebrow. "I don't have all day."

"You could write me a check this instant," she protested. "Why make me jump through hoops?"

"Maybe because I can."

He was being a bastard. He knew it. And by the look on Lucy's face, she knew it, as well. But the opportunity to make her bend to his will was irresistible.

The fact that each of them could still elicit strong emotions from the other should have been a red flag. But then again, that was the story of their relationship. Though he and Lucy had grown up in the same town, they hadn't really known each other. Not until she'd come home to Royal for a lengthy visit after college graduation.

Lucy's parents had been dead by then. Instead of bunking with her cousin Kenny, Lucy had stayed with her childhood friend and college roommate, Kirsten. One of Kirsten's friends had thrown a hello-to-summer bash, and that's where Jeff had met the luscious Lucy.

He still remembered the moment she'd walked into the room. It was a case of instant lust…at least on his part. She was exactly the kind of woman he liked… tall, confident, and with a wicked sense of humor. The two of them had found a private corner and flirted for three hours.

A week later, they'd ended up in bed together.

Unfortunately, their whirlwind courtship and speedy five-month trip to the altar had ended in disaster. Ironically, if they had followed through with their wedding, two days from now would have been their anniversary.

Did Lucy realize the bizarre coincidence?

She stood up and walked to the foyer. "I have to go." The words were tossed over her shoulder, as if she couldn't wait to get out of his house.

He shrugged and followed her, putting a hand high on the door to keep her from escaping. "I don't want to make a trip out to the farm for nothing. So don't try standing me up. If you want the money, you'll get it on my terms or not at all."

Six

Lucy hurried to her car, heartsick and panicked. Why had she ever thought she could appeal to Jeff Hartley's sense of right and wrong? The man was a scoundrel. She was so angry with herself…angry for approaching him in the first place, and even angrier that apparently she was still desperately in love with him…despite everything he had done.

During the past two years, she had firmly purged her emotional system of memories connected to Jeff Hartley. Never once did she think of the way his arms pulled her tight against his broad chest. Or the silkiness of his always rumpled hair. At night in bed, she surely didn't remember how wonderful it was to feel him slide on top of her and into her, their breath mingling in ragged gasps and groans of pleasure.

Stupid man. She parked haphazardly at the farm and

went in search of her cousin. She found him in the barn repairing a harness.

Kenny looked up when she entered. "Hey, Luce. What's up?"

She plopped down on a bale of hay. "How much would it take for you not to sell the land?"

He frowned. "What do you mean? Are you trying to buy it for yourself?"

"Gosh, no. I'd be a terrible farmer. But I have a gut feeling you'll change your mind down the road. And I'm willing to keep things running while you sow your wild oats. So I'm asking…would twenty grand be enough to bankroll your move to LA and get you started? It would be a loan. You'd have to pay back half eventually, and I'll pay back the other half as a thank-you for not letting go of Peyton land."

The frown grew deeper. "A loan from whom?"

Kenny might pretend to be a goofball when it suited him, but the boy was smart…and he knew his grammar.

"From a friend of mine," she said. "No big deal."

Kenny perched on the bale of hay beside hers and put an arm around her shoulders. "What have you done, Luce?"

She sniffed, trying not to cry. "Made a deal with the devil?"

"Are you asking me or telling me?"

Kenny was two years younger than she was. Most of the time she felt like his mother. But for the moment, it was nice to have someone to lean on. "I think Jeff Hartley is going to loan it to me."

"Hell, no." Kenny jumped to his feet, raking both hands through his hair agitatedly. "The man cheated on you and broke your heart. I won't take his money.

We'll think of something else. Or I'll convince you it's okay to sell the farm."

"You'll never convince me of that. What if being an actor doesn't pan out?"

"Do you realize how patronizing you sound, Luce? No offense, but what I want to do is more serious than *sowing wild oats*."

She rubbed her temples with her fingertips. "I shouldn't have said that. I'm sorry."

After a few moments, he went back to repairing the harness. "Why did you go to Jeff, Lucy? Why him?"

Bowing her head, she let the tears fall. "The day after tomorrow would have been our wedding anniversary. Jeff Hartley still owes me for that."

Seven

Jeff made arrangements to have the Hartley Ranch covered, personnel wise, in the event that he didn't return from Midland right away. There was no reason in the world to think that he and Lucy might end up in bed together, but he was a planner. A former Boy Scout. Preparation was second nature to him.

As he went about his business, his mind raced on a far more intimate track. Lucy had betrayed the wedding vows she and Jeff had both written. Before they'd ever made it to the altar. And yet she thought Jeff was the one at fault. Even from the perspective of two years down the road, he was still angry about that.

At four o'clock, he showered and quickly packed a bag. He traveled often for cattle shows and other business-related trips, so he was accustomed to the drill. Then he went online and ordered a variety of items and had them delivered to his favorite hotel.

When he was satisfied that his plans were perfectly in order, he loaded the car, stopped by the bank, and then drove out to the farm. There was at least a fifty-fifty chance Lucy would shut the door in his face. But he was convinced her request for a loan was legit. In order to get the cash, she had to go along with his wishes.

Unfortunately, Kenny answered the door. And he was spoiling for a fight.

Jeff had spent his entire life in Texas. He was no stranger to brawls and the occasional testosterone over-load. But if he had plans for himself and Lucy, first he had to get past her gatekeeper. He held up his hands in the universal gesture for noncombative behavior. "I come in peace, big guy."

"Luce never should have asked you for the money. I can manage on my own."

"In LA? I don't think so. Not without liquidating your assets. And that will break your cousin's heart. Is that really what you want to do?"

"You're hardly the man to talk about breaking Lucy's heart." But it was said without heat. As if Kenny understood that more was at stake here than his would-be career.

"Where is she?" Jeff asked. "We need to go."

"I think she was on the phone, but she'll be out soon. Though I sure as hell don't know why."

"Lucy and I have some unfinished business from two years ago. It's time to settle a few scores."

Kenny blanched. "I don't want to be in the middle of this."

"Too late. You shouldn't have tried to sell your land

to Samson Oil. And besides, Lucy came to me...not the other way around. What does that tell you?"

Kenny bristled. "It tells me that my cousin cares about me. I have no idea what it says about you."

Eight

Lucy stood just out of sight in the hallway and listened to the two men argue. Strangely, there was not much real anger in the exchange. At one time, Kenny and Jeff had been good friends. Kenny was supposed to walk Lucy down the aisle and hand her over to the rancher who had swept her off her feet. But that moment never happened.

Lucy cleared her throat and eased past Kenny to step onto the porch. "Don't worry if I'm late," she said.

Kenny tugged her wrist and leaned in to kiss her on the cheek. "Text me and let me know your plans. So I don't worry."

His droll attempt to play mother hen made her smile. "Very funny. But yes… I'll be in touch."

At last she had to face Jeff. He stood a few feet away, his expression inscrutable. In a dark tailored suit, with a crisp white dress shirt and blue patterned tie, he looked like a man in charge of his domain. A light breeze ruffled his hair.

His sharp, intimate gaze scanned her from head to toe. "Let's go" was all he said.

Lucy sighed inwardly. So much for her sexy black cocktail dress with spaghetti straps. The daring bodice showcased her cleavage nicely. Big surly rancher barely seemed to notice.

They descended the steps side by side, Jeff's hand on her elbow. He helped her into the car, closed her door and went around to slide into the driver's seat. The car was not one she remembered. But it had all the bells and whistles. It smelled of leather and even more faintly, the essence of the man himself.

For the first ten miles silence reigned. Pastures of cattle whizzed by outside the window, their existence so commonplace, Lucy couldn't pretend a deep interest in the scenery. Instead, she kicked off her shoes, curled her legs beneath her, and leaned forward to turn on the satellite radio.

"Do you mind?" she asked.

Jeff shot her a glance. "Does being alone with me make you nervous, Lucy?"

"Of course not." Her hand hovered over the knob. More than anything else, she wanted music to fill the awkward silence. But if Jeff saw that as a sign of weakness, then she wouldn't do it.

She sat back, biting her bottom lip. Now the silence was worse. Before, they had simply been two near strangers riding down the road. Jeff's deliberately provocative question set her nerves on edge.

"While we're on our way," she said, "why don't you

tell me what these conditions are? The ones I have to agree to so you'll loan me the money?"

Jeff didn't answer her question. "I'm curious. Why doesn't Kenny go out and get his own loan?"

"He's shoveled everything he has back into the farm. His credit's maxed out. Besides, his solution is selling to Samson Oil. I explained that."

"True. You did."

"So tell me, Jeff. What do you want from me?"

Nine

What do you want from me? Lucy's frustrated question was one Jeff would have been glad to answer. In detail. Slowly. All night. But first there were hurdles to jump.

Though he kept his hands on the wheel and his eyes on the road, he had already memorized every nuance of his companion's appearance. Everything from her sexy black high heels all the way up to her sleek and shiny hair tucked behind one ear.

Her black cocktail dress, at first glance, was entirely appropriate for dinner in the big city. But damned if he wasn't going to have the urge to take off his jacket and wrap her up in it. He didn't want other men looking at her.

He felt possessive, which was ridiculous, because Lucy was definitely her own woman. If she chose to prance stark naked down Main Street, he couldn't stop her. So maybe he needed to take a different tack entirely. Instead of bossing her around, perhaps he should use another very enjoyable means of communication.

Right now, she was a hen with ruffled feathers. He had upset her already. The truth was, he didn't care. He'd rather have anger from Lucy than outright indifference.

He could work with anger.

"We'll talk about the specifics over dinner, Lucy. Why don't you relax and tell me about your work in Austin."

His diversion worked for the next half hour. In his peripheral vision, he watched as Lucy's body language went from tense and guarded to normal. Or at least as normal as it could be given the history between them.

Later, when he pulled up in front of the luxury hotel in the heart of the city, Lucy shot him a sharp-eyed glance.

He took her elbow and led her inside. "The restaurant here is phenomenal," he said. "I think you'll enjoy it."

Over appetizers and drinks, Lucy thawed further. "So far, I'm impressed. I forgot to eat lunch today, so I was starving."

Jeff was hungry, too, but he barely tasted the food. He was gambling a hell of a lot on the outcome of this encounter.

They ordered the works…filet and lobster. With spinach salad and crusty rolls. Clearly, Lucy enjoyed her meal. *He* enjoyed the fact that she didn't fuss about calories and instead ate with enthusiasm.

Good food prepared from fresh ingredients was a sensual experience. It tapped into some of the same pleasure centers as lovemaking. It was hard to bicker under the influence of a really exceptional Chablis and a satisfying, special-occasion dinner.

That's what he was counting on...

Lucy declined dessert. Jeff did, as well. As they lingered over coffee, he could practically see her girding her loins for battle.

She stirred a single packet of sugar into her cup and sat back in her chair, eyeing him steadily. "Enough stalling, Jeff. I've come here with you for dinner, which was amazing, I might add. But I need to have your answer. Will you loan me the money, and what are your conditions?"

Ten

Lucy was braced for bad news. It was entirely possible that Jeff had brought her here—wined and dined her—in order to let her down gently. To give her an outright no.

Watching him take a sip of coffee was only one of many mistakes she had made tonight. When his lips made contact with the rim of his thin china cup, she was almost sure the world stood still for a split second. The man had the most amazing mouth. Firm lips that could caress a woman's breast or kiss her senseless in the space of a heartbeat.

Though it had been two long years, Lucy still remembered the taste of his tongue on hers.

"Jeff?" She heard the impatience in her voice. "I asked you a question."

He nodded slowly. "Okay. Hear me out before you run screaming from the room."

Her nape prickled. "I don't understand."

Leaning toward her, he rested his forearms on the table, hands clasped in front of him. His dark gaze captured hers like a mesmerist. "When you walked out the night before our wedding, we never had closure. I went from being almost married to drastically single so fast it's a wonder I didn't get whiplash."

"What's your point?" Her throat was tight.

"Divorced couples end up back in bed together all the time. Lovers break up and hook up and break up again. I'm curious to see if you and I still have a spark."

Hyperventilation threatened. "We can talk about that later." *Much later.* "You said you had two conditions. What are they?" For the first time tonight, she caught a glimpse of something in his eyes. Was it pain? Or vulnerability? Not likely.

He shrugged. "I want you to ask Kirsten to tell you what really happened that night."

"I don't need to talk to Kirsten. I'm not blind. I saw everything. You kissed her and she kissed you back. Both of you betrayed me. The truth is, Kirsten and I have barely spoken since that night. She has shut me out. I think she's embarrassed that she didn't stop you."

"And you really believe that?"

His tone wasn't sarcastic. If anything, the words were wistful, cajoling. She'd spent two horrid years wondering why the man who professed to love her madly had been such a jerk. Or why Kirsten, her best friend, hadn't punched Jeff in the stomach. She had seen Kirsten's face when Lucy caught them. The other woman had looked shattered. But her arms had definitely been twined about Jeff's neck.

"I don't know what to believe anymore," she muttered. Jeff hadn't dated anyone at all in the last twenty-four months according to Royal's gossipy grapevine. He was a young, virile man in his prime. If he was such a lying, cheating scoundrel, why hadn't he been out on the town with a dozen women in the interim? "And if I do go talk to Kirsten about what happened? That's it? What about the other requirement?"

Those chiseled lips curved upward in a smile that made her spine tighten and her stomach curl. "I'd like the two of us to go upstairs and spend the night together."

Eleven

Go upstairs and spend the night together.

His words echoed in her brain like tiny pinballs. "You mean sex?"

Jeff laughed out loud, but it was gentle laughter, and his eyes were filled with warmth. "Yes, Lucy. Sex. I've missed you. I've missed us."

Oh, my...

What was a woman supposed to say to that kind of proposition? Especially when it sounded so very appealing. She cleared her throat. "If you're offering to pay me twenty thousand dollars to have sex with you, I think we could both get arrested."

His smile was enigmatic. "Let's not muddy the waters, then. I promise to give you the money for Kenny as long as you have a conversation with Kirsten." He reached across the table and took one of her hands in both of his. When he rubbed his thumb across her wrist, it was all she could do not to jerk away in a panic.

"Steady, Lucy." His grip tightened. "I think deep in your heart you know the truth. But you're afraid to face it. I understand that. Maybe it will take time. So for tonight, I'm not expecting you to make any sweeping declarations. I'm only asking if you'll be my lover again. One night. For closure. Unless you change your mind and decide you want more."

"Why would I do that?" she asked faintly, remembering all the evenings she had cried herself to sleep.

"You'll have to figure it out for yourself," he said. That same thumb rubbed back and forth across her knuckles.

She seized on one inescapable truth. "But I don't have anything with me to stay overnight," she said, grasping at straws. "And neither do you."

"I brought a bag," he replied calmly. "And I ordered a few items for a female companion. I believe you'll find I've thought of everything you need to be comfortable."

"And you don't think this is at all creepy?" With her free hand she picked up her water glass, intending to take a sip. But her fingers shook so much she set it back down immediately.

Jeff released her, his expression sober. "You're the one who came to see me, not the other way around. If you want me to take you home, all you have to do is say so. But I'm hoping you'll give us this one night to see if the spark is still there."

"Why are you doing this?" she whispered. He was breaking her heart all over again, and she was so damned afraid to trust him. Even worse, she was afraid to trust herself.

Jeff summoned the waiter and dealt with the check. Moments later, the transaction was complete. Jeff stood and held out his hand. "I need your decision, Lucy." He was tall and sexy and clear-eyed in his resolve. "Shall we go, or shall we stay? It's up to you. It always has been."

Twelve

Jeff's heartbeat thundered in his chest. He wasn't usually much of a gambler, but he was betting on a future that, at the moment, didn't exist.

It was a thousand years before Lucy slid her small hand into his bigger one. "Yes," she said. The word was barely audible.

He led her among the crowded tables and out into the hotel foyer. After tucking her into an elegant wing-back chair, he brushed a finger across her cheek. "Stay here. I won't be long."

Perhaps the desk clerk thought him a tad weird. Jeff could barely register for glancing back over his shoulder to see if Lucy had bolted. But all was well. She had her phone in her hand and was apparently checking messages.

When he had the key, he went back for her. "Ready?"

Her face was pale when she looked up at him. But she smiled and rose to her feet. "Yes."

They shared an elevator with three other people. On the seventh floor, Jeff took Lucy's arm and steered her off. "This way," he said gruffly as he located their room number on the brass placard. They were at the end of the hall, far from the noise of the elevator and the ice machine.

He'd booked a suite. Inside the pleasantly neutral sitting room, he took off his jacket and tie. "Would you like more wine?" he asked.

Lucy hovered by the door. "No. Why do you want me to go talk to Kirsten?" Her eyes were huge…perhaps revealing distress over the shambles of their past.

He leaned against the arm of the sofa. "She was your friend from childhood. You and I had dated less than a year. As angry as I was with you, on some level I understood."

"Why were you angry with *me*?" she asked, her expression bewildered. "You were the one who cheated."

He didn't rise to the bait. "It's been two years, Lucy. Two long, frustrating years when you and I should have been starting our life together. Surely you've had time enough to figure it out by now."

"You didn't come after me." Her voice was small, the tone wounded.

Ah…there it was. The evidence of his own stupidity. "You're right about that. I let my pride get in the way. When you wouldn't take my calls, I wanted to make you grovel. But as it turns out, that was an abysmally arrogant and unproductive attitude on my part. I'm sorry I didn't follow you back to Austin. I should have.

Maybe one good knock-down, drag-out fight would have cleared the air."

"And now…if I agree to go talk to Kirsten?"

He swallowed the last of his wine and set the glass aside. "I don't want to discuss Kirsten anymore. You and I are the only two people here in this suite. What I desperately need is make love to you."

Thirteen

Lucy sucked in a deep breath, her insides tumbling as they had the one and only time she rode the Tilt-A-Whirl at the county fair. On that occasion, she had tossed her cookies afterward.

Tonight was different. Tonight, the butterflies were all about anticipation and arousal and the rebirth of hope. Why else would she be here with Jeff Hartley?

She nodded, kicking off her shoes. "Yes." There were a million words she wanted to say to him, and not all of them kind. But for some reason, the only thing that mattered at this very moment was feeling the warmth of his skin beneath her fingers one more time.

She felt more emotionally bereft than brave, but she made her feet move…carrying her across the plush carpet until she stood face-to-face with Jeff. His gaze was stormy, his fists were clenched at his sides.

He stared into her eyes as if looking for something he was afraid he wouldn't find. "God, you're beautiful," he said, his voice hoarse. "I thought I could put you out of my mind, but that was laughable. You've haunted every room in my house. Kiss me, Lucy."

With one of his strong arms around her back, binding her to him, she went up on her tiptoes and found his mouth with hers. The taste of him brought tears to sting her eyelids, but she blinked them back, wanting this moment to be about light and warmth and pleasure. He held her gently as he took everything she thought she knew and stripped it away, leaving only a yearning that was heart-deep and visceral.

She wanted to say something, but Jeff was a man possessed. He found the zipper at her back and lowered it with one smooth move. Then he shimmied the garment down her body and held her arm as she stepped out of the small heap of fabric.

Beneath the dress, she wore lacy underthings. Jeff didn't pause to admire them. The lingerie went the way of the crumpled dress.

Suddenly, she realized that she was completely naked, and her would-be lover was staring. Hotly. Glassy-eyed. As if he'd been struck in the head and was seeing stars.

She crossed her arms over strategic areas and scowled. "Take off your clothes, Mr. Hartley. This show works both ways."

If the situation hadn't been so emotionally fraught, she might have chuckled when Jeff dragged his shirt, still half-buttoned, over his head. His pants and socks and shoes were next in the frenzied disrobing.

Underneath, he wore snug-fitting black boxers that

strained to contain his arousal. Suddenly, she felt shy and afraid and clueless. Had she ever really known this man at all?

He didn't give her time for second thoughts. "We'll be more comfortable on the bed," he promised, scooping her up and carrying her through the adjacent doorway. She barely noticed the furnishings or the color scheme. Her gaze was locked on Jeff's face.

His cheekbones were slashed with color. His eyes glittered with lust. "You're mine, Lucy."

Fourteen

The bottom dropped out of her stomach. It was as simple as that. Even if he hadn't said the words, she would have felt his deep conviction in the way he moved his hands over her body.

He still wore his underwear, maybe to keep things from rushing along too rapidly. He was tanned all over from his days of working in the hot sun. His chest was a work of art, sleekly muscled…lightly dusted with golden hair.

Even as she took in the magnificence that was Jeff Hartley, she couldn't help but question his motives. As a rancher and a member of the Texas Cattleman's Club in Royal, he was a well-respected member of the community. Had his reputation suffered when she walked out on him? Was there a part of him that wanted revenge?

He loomed over her on one elbow, his emerald eyes

darker than normal, his forehead damp, his skin hot.
It was all she could do to be still and let him map her
curves like a blind man. Need rose, hot and torment-
ing, between her clenched thighs.

How could she want him so desperately while knowing full well there were serious unresolved issues between them? "Jeff," she whispered, not really knowing
what to say. "Please…" Despite what her head told her,
her heart and her body were in control.

It was as if they had never been apart. He rolled her
to her stomach and moved aside a swath of her hair to
kiss the nape of her neck. The press of his lips against
sensitive skin sent sparkles of sensation all down to
her feet.

When he nibbled his way along her spine, her hands
grabbed the sheets. He lay heavy against her, his big
body weighing her down deliciously.

At last she felt him move away. He scrambled out of
his boxers and rolled her to face him once again. She
let her arms fall lax above her head, enjoying the way
his avid gaze scoured her from head to toe.

It had been two years since she had seen him naked…
two years since she had seen him at all. Beginning with
what would have been their wedding morning, he had
phoned her every single day for a week. Each one of
those times she had let his call go to voice mail, telling
herself he should have had the guts to face her in person.

Had she wronged him grievously? In her blind hurt,
had she rushed to judgment? The enormity of the question made her head spin.

For weeks and months, she had wallowed in her self-
righteous anger, calling Jeff Hartley every dirty name

in the book, telling herself she hated him...that he was a worthless cad, a two-timing player.

But what if she had been wrong? What if she had been terribly, dreadfully wrong?

He used his thumb to erase the frown lines between her brows. "What's the matter, buttercup?"

Hearing the silly nickname made the lump in her throat grow larger. "I don't know what we're doing, Jeff."

His smile was lopsided, more rueful than happy. "Damned if I know either. But let's worry about that tomorrow."

She cupped his cheek, feeling the light stubble of late-day beard. "Since when do *you* channel Scarlett O'Hara?"

Without answering, he reached in his discarded pants for a condom and took care of business. Then he moved between her thighs. "Put your arms around my neck, Lucy. I want to feel you skin to skin."

Fifteen

Jeff tried to live an honorable life. He gave to charity, offered work to those who needed it, supported his local civic organizations and donated large sums of money to the church where he had been baptized as an infant.

But lying in Lucy's arms, on the brink of restaking a claim that had lain dormant for two years, he would have sold his soul to the devil if he could have frozen time.

Lucy's eyes were closed.

"Look at me," he commanded. "I want you to see my face when I take you."

Her breath came in short, sharp pants. She nodded, her eyelids fluttering upward as she obeyed.

Gently, he spread her thighs and positioned his aching flesh against the moist, pink lips of her sex. When he pushed inside, he was pretty sure he blacked out for a moment. *Two years. Two damn years.*

It was everything he remembered and more. The fragrance of her silky skin. The sound of her soft, incoherent cries. His body and his soul would have recognized her even in the dark, anywhere in the world.

He felt her heart beating against his chest. Or maybe it was his heart. It was impossible to separate the two. Burying his face in the crook of her shoulder, he moved in her steadily, sucking in a sharp breath when she wrapped her legs around his waist, driving him deeper.

He thrust slowly at first, but all the willpower in the world couldn't stem the tide of his hunger. His body betrayed him, his desire cresting sharply in a release that left him almost insensate.

Lucy hadn't come. He knew that. But his embarrassment was blunted by the sheer euphoria of being with her again. He kissed her cheek. "I'm sorry, love." He touched her gently, intimately, stroking and teasing until she climaxed, too. Afterward, he held her close for long minutes.

But reality eventually intruded.

Lucy reclined on her elbow, head propped on her hand. "May I ask you a very personal question?"

Though his breathing was still far from steady, he nodded. "Anything."

Lucy reached out and smoothed a lock of his hair. Her gaze was troubled. "When was the last time you had sex?"

Here it was. The first test of their tenuous reconciliation. "You should know," he said quietly. "You were there."

She went white, her expression anguished, tears spilling from her eyes and rolling down her cheeks. "You're lying," she whispered.

Her accusation angered him. But he gathered her into his arms and held her as she sobbed. Two years of grief and separation. Two years of lost happiness.

"I know you don't believe me, Lucy." He combed her hair with his fingers. "Maybe you never will. Don't cry so hard. You'll make yourself sick."

Perhaps they should have talked first. But his need for her had obliterated everything else. Now she was distraught, and he didn't know how to help her get to the truth. Was this going to be the only moment they had? If so, he wasn't prepared to let it end so soon.

Feeling her nude body against his healed the raw places inside him. She was his. He would fight. For however long it took. No matter what happened, he was never letting her go again.

Sixteen

Lucy's brain whirled in sickening circles. Jeff wanted her to believe he hadn't been with another woman since she walked out on him. He expected her to believe he had not cheated on her.

She should have been elated…relieved. Instead, she was shattered and confused and overwhelmed. Was she going to be one of those women who blindly accepted whatever her lover told her? Where was her pride? Her intuition? Her intellect?

Jeff was silent, but tense. She knew him well enough to realize that he was angry. Even so, the strong arms holding her close were her only anchors at a moment when everything she thought she knew was shattering into tiny fragments and swirling away.

At last, the storm of grief passed. She lay against him limp with emotional distress. Taking a deep breath, she tried to sit up. "We need to go back to Royal. Right now. I need to see you and Kirsten in the same room at the same time to hash this out."

Jeff moved up against the headboard. His jaw was tight, but he scooped her into his lap. "It can wait until tomorrow. We deserve this night together, Lucy. You and I. No one else. Even if you don't believe me."

With her cheek against his chest, she seesawed between hope and despair. Was it possible she hadn't lost him after all, or was she being a credulous fool? If she had placed more trust in what they had from the beginning, it might never have come to this. Was it too late to repair the damage and to reclaim the future that had almost been destroyed?

And what if Jeff *had* initiated the kiss with Kirsten? Could she forgive him and move on? Was what they had worth another chance? Would their relationship ever be the same?

She was deeply moved, unbearably regretful, and at the same time giddy with hope. Tipping back her head so she could see his face, she memorized his features. The heavy-lidded green eyes. The strong chin. The slightly crooked nose. The tiny scar below his left cheekbone.

He gazed down at her with a half-smile. "Are we good?"

"I'm not sure." She wanted to say more. She wanted to pour out her heart...to tell him about the endless months of despair and loneliness. But now was not the time to be sad. "Kiss me again," she whispered unsteadily. "So I know this isn't a dream."

Jeff leaned her over his arm and gave her what she asked for, warm and slow...soft and deep. With each fractured sigh on her part and every ragged groan from him, arousal shimmered and spread until every cell of her body pulsed wildly with wanting him. She grabbed handfuls of his hair, trying to drag him closer.

He winced and laughed. "Easy, darlin'. I don't want to go bald just yet."

His trademark humor was one of the things that had attracted her to him in the beginning. That and his broad-shouldered, lanky body.

Before she knew what was happening, he had levered her onto her back and was leaning over her, shaping the curves of her breasts with his fingertips. Her nipples were so sensitive, she could hardly stand for him to touch them.

"I need you inside me again," she pleaded.

"Not yet." His smile was feral. "Have patience, Lucy, love. We've got all night."

Seventeen

Jeff wanted to worship her body and mark it as his and drive her insane with pleasure. It was a tall order for a man still wrung out from his own release. Not that he wasn't ready for another round. He was. He definitely was. His erection throbbed with a hunger that wouldn't be sated anytime soon.

But somehow he had to make Lucy understand.

When he tasted the tips of her breasts, circled the areolas with his tongue, she gasped and arched her back. He pressed her to the mattress and moved south, teasing her belly button before kissing his way down her hips and thighs and legs one at a time. He even spent a few crazy minutes playing with her toes, and this from a man who had never once entertained a foot fetish.

By this point, she was calling him names…pleading for more.

He laughed, but it was a hoarse laugh. He knew the joke was on him. All his plans to demonstrate how high he could push her evaporated in the driving urge to fill her and erase the memory of every hour that had separated them.

His brain was so fuzzy he only remembered the new condom at the last minute. Once he was ready, he knelt and lifted one of Lucy's legs onto his shoulder. He paused—only a moment—to appreciate the sensual picture she made.

Everything about her was perfect…from the graceful arch of her neck to her narrow waist to the small mole just below her right breast.

He touched her deliberately, stroking the little spot that made her body weep for him. Even though he was gentle and almost lazy in his caress, Lucy climaxed wildly, her release beautiful and real and utterly impossible to resist. "God, I want you," he muttered.

When he thrust inside her, her orgasm hit another peak. The feel of her inner muscles fluttering against his sex drove him to the brink of control. He went still… chest heaving, hips moving restlessly despite his pause.

"Lucy?"

Her teeth dug into her bottom lip. "Yes?"

"I was furious with you for not trusting me. But I never stopped loving you."

"Oh, Jeff…" The look on her face told him she wasn't there yet. She still had doubts. He could wait, maybe. He wanted her to be absolutely sure. For now it was enough to feel…and to know…

Lucy was his.

He retreated and lifted her onto her knees, stuffing pillows beneath her. Her butt was the prettiest thing he'd ever seen, heart-shaped and full. Lucy had bemoaned the curves of her bottom on numerous occasions. Tonight, as he palmed it and squeezed it and steadied himself against it to enter her again with one firm push, he decided he could spend the rest of his life proving to her how perfect it was.

Leaning forward, he gathered her hair into a ponytail, securing it with his fist and using the grip to turn her head. "Look in the mirror, Lucy. This is us. This is real."

Eighteen

Lucy hadn't even noticed that the dresser was conveniently situated across from the bed...and that the mirror faithfully reflected Jeff's sun-bronzed body and her own paler frame. The carnal image was indelibly imprinted on her brain. As long as she lived, she would never forget this moment.

She closed her eyes and bent her head. Jeff released her hair, letting it fall around her face. Behind her, his harsh breathing was audible. At last, he moved with a muffled shout, slamming into her again and again until he shuddered and moaned and slumped on top of her as they both collapsed onto the mattress.

Minutes later...maybe hours, so skewed was her sense of time, she stirred. In the interim, they had untangled their bodies. Jeff lay flat on his back, one arm

flung across his eyes. She snuggled against him, draping her leg across his hairy thigh. "Are you alive?"

"Mmph…"

It wasn't much of a response, but it made her smile.

She danced her fingertips over his rib cage. At one
time, he had been very ticklish.

His face scrunched up and he batted her hand away.
"Five minutes," he begged, the words slurred. "That's
all I need."

"Take your time," she teased. She rested her cheek
against his chest, feeling so light with happiness it was
a wonder she didn't float up to the ceiling. Maybe she
was being naive. Maybe he would hurt her again. But
at the moment, none of that seemed to matter.

"You never gave me a chance to explain two years
ago," he muttered.

His statement dampened her euphoria. "Would it
have mattered? I was desperately hurt and in shock. I'm
not sure anything you said would have gotten through
to me."

"I deserved a fair hearing, Lucy. We were in a committed relationship, but you were too stubborn to be
reasonable."

His eyes were closed, so she couldn't see his expression. But his jaw was tight.

Was it all an act? Jeff playing up his innocence?

There was only one way to know for sure, even if the
prospect curled her stomach. "Will you do me a favor?"
she asked quietly.

Jeff yawned. "The way I feel right now, you could
ask me for the moon and I'd call NASA to help me get
it for you."

She reared up on one elbow and gaped. "Why, Jeff

Hartley! That was the most romantic thing you've ever said to me."

And there it was again. *Doubt.* Many a woman had been swayed by pretty words.

He chuckled, holding her tightly against his side. "I've had two years to practice," he said. "Prepare to be amazed. But let's not get off track. What's this big favor you need from me?"

"Will you go with me to Kirsten's house?"

His entire body froze. "If it's all the same to you, I'd rather not come anywhere near that woman."

She kissed his bicep. "Please. I have to hear the truth. I know you want me to take you on faith, but I need something more concrete. I need you to understand my doubts, and I need your moral support."

"Damn it. That's what I get for promising you the moon."

Nineteen

The following morning when Lucy woke up, she didn't know where she was. And then it all came back to her in a rush of memories from the night before. She and Jeff Hartley had done naughty things in this huge bed. Naughty, wonderful things.

During the night, he had insisted on holding her close as they slept, though in truth, sleep had been far down the list of their favorite activities. Actually, ranking right below mind-blowing sex were the strawberries and champagne they had ordered from room service at 3:00 a.m.

Jeff was still asleep. She studied him unashamedly, feeling her heart swell with hope and then contract with fear. Loving him once had nearly destroyed her. Could she let herself love him again?

She flinched in surprise when the naked man beneath the covers moved and spoke. "I am not a peep show for your private entertainment," he mumbled.

Reaching beneath the sheet, she took him in her hand. "Are you sure?"

What followed was a very pleasant start to their morning. When they were both rumpled and limp with satisfaction, she poked his arm. "Time to put on some clothes and check out. I want to get this over with."

An hour later, they were on the highway, headed back to Royal. Lucy sat rigid in her seat, her hands clenched in her lap. Layers of dread filled her stomach with each passing mile.

When they reached the fringes of Royal proper, Jeff pulled off on the side of the road and turned to face her. "There's something else I need to tell you."

She blanched. "Oh?"

"Nothing bad," he said hastily, correctly reading her state of mind. "I want you to know that I had my bank transfer twenty thousand dollars to Kenny's account before you and I ever made it to Midland. I wanted you and me to be intimate, but only if you wanted it, too."

Lucy shook her head. "Thank you for that." But even as she said the words, she wondered if his generosity might be a ploy to win her trust…to play the knight in shining armor.

Of course, Jeff knew where Kirsten lived. The party where Jeff and Lucy first connected had been down the street from Kirsten's house. When Jeff parked at the curb, Lucy took a deep breath. "This is it, I guess."

Jeff was at her side as they made their way up the walk. Lucy rang the bell. Kirsten herself opened the door…and upon seeing Lucy and Jeff together, immediately turned the color of milk, her expression distraught.

She didn't invite them in. They stood in an awkward trio with the noonday sun beaming down.

Lucy squared her shoulders. "It's been painful having you treat me so coldly these last two years, Kirsten. But I have to know the truth. If Jeff kissed you and you were seduced into responding, I need to hear you admit it."

Kirsten scowled. "What does the sainted Jeff Hartley have to say about the whole mess? I suppose he's told you what a bitch I am…what a terrible friend."

"Actually, he hasn't said much of anything. The man I knew two years ago wouldn't have cheated on me. But the only other explanation is that my best friend deliberately ruined my wedding."

Kirsten wrapped her arms around her waist, her expression hunted. "Why would I do that?"

"I don't know. But I've run out of scenarios, and I'm damned tired of wondering." Kirsten sneered. "Men are pigs. They want what they can't have. Jeff put the moves on me. He cheated on you."

Suddenly, the pain was as fresh as if the incident had happened yesterday. Seeing Kirsten in Jeff's arms had nearly killed Lucy. But now she had to take one of them on faith. Either her childhood friend or her lover.

She stared at Kirsten. "Did *he* cheat on me? Or did *you*?"

It was a standoff two years in the making. No matter what the answer turned out to be, Lucy lost someone she cared about, someone she loved.

Jeff remained silent during the long, dreadful seconds that elapsed. Time settled into slow motion…

At last, Kirsten's face crumpled. Her eyes flashed

with a combination of guilt and anger. "If you'd had more faith in him, nothing I did would have mattered."

Lucy gasped, struck by the truth in the accusation. But her own behavior wasn't on trial at the moment. Shock paralyzed her, despite the part of her that must have accepted the truth somewhere deep down inside. "So it's true?" Lucy spared one glance at Jeff, but he was stone-faced.

Kirsten shrugged. "It's true. Your precious Jeff is innocent."

Lucy trembled. Knowing was one thing. Hearing it bluntly stated out loud was painful…and baffling. "Why, Kirsten? I have to know why?"

Kirsten was almost defiant now. "I was jealous. Ever since we were kids, things seemed so easy for you. When we came back from college and you hooked up with Jeff at the party, I was furious. I'd had my eye on him for a long time."

Lucy shook her head in disbelief. "You were so popular, Kirsten. I don't even know what you mean."

Kirsten shrugged. "I hoarded my resentment. Everything came to a head the night of your rehearsal dinner. I saw my chance and I took it. I kissed Jeff. Because I knew you were right outside the door. He had nothing to do with it."

"Oh, Kirsten. You were my best friend."

The other woman shook her head. "But not anymore." Quietly, Kirsten closed the door.

Twenty

Jeff took Lucy's arm and steered her back toward the car. "Give her time," he said. "The two of you may get beyond this."

Lucy stared at him. "How can you be so calm?"

He caressed her cheek, his eyes filled with warmth. "I have you back in my life again, Lucy. Nothing can hurt me now."

"Take me home with you, Jeff. Please."

They made the trip in silence. Her thoughts were in shambles. How had she been so wrong about so many things?

In Jeff's living room, she prowled. He leaned a shoulder against the doorframe, his gaze following her around the room. At last, he sighed. "Sometimes we have to put the past behind us, sweetheart. We have to choose to be happy and move on."

At last, Lucy stood in front of him, hands on her hips. "I love you, too, Jeff. I'm sorry I didn't trust you…that I didn't trust us. Kirsten had been my friend since we were nine years old. When I saw her in your arms, it didn't make sense. So my default was to doubt you. And maybe to doubt myself, too, because I fell in love with you so quickly." She took a deep breath. "I adore you. I suppose I'll have to spend the rest of my life making this up to you."

He pulled her close and kissed her hard, making her heart skip several beats. "Nonsense. We're not going to talk about it again. Today is our new beginning."

Even in the midst of an almost miraculous second chance, Lucy fretted. "There's one more thing."

He scooped her into his arms and carried her to the sofa, sprawling with her in his arms. "Go ahead," he said, his tone resigned.

"I don't want people to gossip about us. Can we please keep this quiet? At least until after Christmas? That will give me time to go back to Austin and turn in my notice. I'll have to sell my condo if I'm coming back to run the farm. I'll convince Kenny to turn down the Samson Oil offer and stick around until the new year."

Jeff's eyes narrowed…giving him the look of a really pissed off cowboy. "No way," he said, his jaw thrust out. "We're getting married this week. I'm not stupid."

She petted his shirtfront. "Then go with me to Austin," she said urgently. "We'll have a quiet wedding at the courthouse. Just you and me. But nobody has to know. I want time for us to be us." She kissed his chin. "You understand, don't you?"

He moved her beneath him on the sofa, unzipping her black pants and toying with the lacy edge of her undies. "As long as you're in my bed every night, I'll do whatever you want, Lucy. But I won't wait to put my ring on your finger."

She linked her arms around his neck, drawing his head down so she could kiss him. "Whatever you say, cowboy. I'm all yours."

* * * * *

Don't miss a single installment of
TEXAS CATTLEMAN'S CLUB:
LIES AND LULLABIES

*Baby secrets and a scheming
sheikh rock Royal, Texas*

COURTING THE COWBOY BOSS
by USA TODAY *bestselling author Janice Maynard*

LONE STAR HOLIDAY PROPOSAL
by USA TODAY *bestselling author Yvonne Lindsay*

NANNY MAKES THREE
by Cat Schield

THE DOCTOR'S BABY DARE
by USA TODAY *bestselling author Michelle Celmer*

THE SEAL'S SECRET HEIRS
by Kat Cantrell

A SURPRISE FOR THE SHEIKH
by Sarah M. Anderson

IN PURSUIT OF HIS WIFE
by Kristi Gold

A BRIDE FOR THE BOSS
by USA TODAY *bestselling author Maureen Child*

*If you're on Twitter, tell us what you think
of Harlequin Desire! #harlequindesire*

#2413 BANE

The Westmorelands • by Brenda Jackson

Rancher and military hero Bane Westmoreland is on a mission to reconnect with the one who got away—his estranged wife. And when the beautiful chemist's discovery puts her in danger, Bane vows to protect her at all costs...

#2414 TRIPLETS UNDER THE TREE

Billionaires and Babies • by Kat Cantrell

A plane crash took his memory. But then billionaire fighter Antonio Cavallari makes it home for the holidays only to discover the triplets he never knew...and their very off-limits, very tempting surrogate mother.

#2415 LONE STAR HOLIDAY PROPOSAL

Texas Cattleman's Club: Lies and Lullabies
by Yvonne Lindsay

At risk of losing her business, single mother Raina Patterson finds solace in the arms of Texas deal-maker Nolan Dane. But does this mysterious stranger have a hidden agenda that will put her heart at even bigger risk?

#2416 A WHITE WEDDING CHRISTMAS

Brides and Belles • by Andrea Laurence

When a cynical wedding planner is forced to work with her teenage crush to plan his sister's Christmas wedding, sparks fly! But will she finally find a happily-ever-after of her own with this second-chance man?

#2417 THE RANCHER'S SECRET SON

Lone Star Legends • by Sara Orwig

For wealthy rancher Nick Milan, hearing the woman he loved and lost tell him he's a daddy is the shock of a lifetime. The revelation could derail his political career...or put the real prize back within tantalizing reach...

#2418 TAKING THE BOSS TO BED

by Joss Wood

After producer Ryan Jackson kisses a stranger to save her from his client's unwanted attentions, he realizes she's actually his newest employee! Faking a relationship is now essential for business, but soon real passion becomes the bottom line...

REQUEST YOUR FREE BOOKS!
2 FREE NOVELS PLUS 2 FREE GIFTS!

H HARLEQUIN®

Desire

ALWAYS POWERFUL, PASSIONATE AND PROVOCATIVE

YES! Please send me 2 FREE Harlequin® Desire novels and my 2 FREE gifts (gifts are worth about $10). After receiving them, if I don't wish to receive any more books, I can return the shipping statement marked "cancel." If I don't cancel, I will receive 6 brand-new novels every month and be billed just $4.55 per book in the U.S. or $5.24 per book in Canada. That's a savings of at least 13% off the cover price! It's quite a bargain! Shipping and handling is just 50¢ per book in the U.S. and 75¢ per book in Canada.* I understand that accepting the 2 free books and gifts places me under no obligation to buy anything. I can always return a shipment and cancel at any time. Even if I never buy another book, the two free books and gifts are mine to keep forever.

225/326 HDN GH2P

Name _____ (PLEASE PRINT) _____

Address _____ Apt. # _____

City _____ State/Prov. _____ Zip/Postal Code _____

Signature (if under 18, a parent or guardian must sign)

Mail to the **Reader Service:**
IN U.S.A.: P.O. Box 1867, Buffalo, NY 14240-1867
IN CANADA: P.O. Box 609, Fort Erie, Ontario L2A 5X3

Want to try two free books from another line?
Call 1-800-873-8635 or visit www.ReaderService.com.

* Terms and prices subject to change without notice. Prices do not include applicable taxes. Sales tax applicable in N.Y. Canadian residents will be charged applicable taxes. Offer not valid in Quebec. This offer is limited to one order per household. Not valid for current subscribers to Harlequin Desire books. All orders subject to credit approval. Credit or debit balances in a customer's account(s) may be offset by any other outstanding balance owed by or to the customer. Please allow 4 to 6 weeks for delivery. Offer available while quantities last.

Your Privacy—The Reader Service is committed to protecting your privacy. Our Privacy Policy is available online at www.ReaderService.com or upon request from the Reader Service.

We make a portion of our mailing list available to reputable third parties that offer products we believe may interest you. If you prefer that we not exchange your name with third parties, or if you wish to clarify or modify your communication preferences, please visit us at www.ReaderService.com/consumerschoice or write to us at Reader Service Preference Service, P.O. Box 9062, Buffalo, NY 14240-9062. Include your complete name and address.

HD15

*Bane Westmoreland and Crystal Newsome secretly
eloped when they were young—but then their families
tore them apart. Now, five years later, Bane is coming
back for his woman, and no one will stop him.*

*Read on for a sneak peek of BANE
the final book in Brenda Jackson's
THE WESTMORELAND series*

With her heart thundering hard in her chest, Crystal
began throwing items in the suitcase open on her bed.
Had she imagined it or had she been watched when she'd
entered her home tonight? She had glanced around several
times and hadn't noticed anything or anyone. But still…

She took a deep breath, knowing she couldn't lose her
cool. She made a decision to leave her car here and a few
lights burning inside her house to give the impression she
was home. She would call a cab to take her to the airport
and would take only the necessities and a few items of
clothing. She could buy anything else she needed.

But this, she thought as she studied the photo album
she held in her hand, went everywhere with her. She had
purchased it right after her last phone call with Bane.
Her parents had sent Crystal to live with Aunt Rachel to
finish out the last year of school. They wanted to get her
away from Bane, not knowing she and Bane had secretly
married.

A couple of months after she left Denver, she'd gotten
a call from him. He'd told her he'd enlisted in the navy

because he needed to grow up, become responsible and make something out of himself. She deserved a man who could be all that he could be, and after he'd accomplished that goal he would come for her. Sitting on the edge of the bed now, she flipped through the album, which she had dedicated to Bane. She thought of him often. Every day. What she tried not to think about was why it was taking him so long to come back for her, or how he might be somewhere enjoying life without her. Forcing those thoughts from her mind, she packed the album in her luggage.

Moments later, she had rolled her luggage into the living room and was calling for a cab when her doorbell rang.

She went still. Nobody ever visited her. Who would be doing so now? She crept back into the shadows of her hallway, hoping whoever was at the door would think she wasn't home. She held her breath when the doorbell sounded again. Did the person on the other side know she was there?

She rushed into her bedroom and grabbed her revolver out of the nightstand drawer. By the time she'd made it back to the living room, there was a second knock. She moved toward the door, but stopped five feet away. "Who is it?" She tightened her hands on the revolver.

There was a moment of silence. And then a voice said, "It's me, Crystal. Bane."

Bane will do whatever it takes to keep his woman safe, but will it be enough?

Don't miss BANE by New York Times *bestselling author Brenda Jackson. Available December 2015 wherever Harlequin® Desire books and ebooks are sold.*

www.Harlequin.com

HARLEQUIN *Desire*

This Christmas, he'll meet his three babies for the first time... and desire their mother in a whole new way!

A plane crash took his memory. But then billionaire fighter Antonio Cavallari makes it home for the holidays only to discover the triplets he never knew...and their very off-limits, very tempting surrogate mother.

Triplets Under the Tree is part of Harlequin Desire's #1 bestselling series, **Billionaires and Babies**: Powerful men... wrapped around their babies' little fingers.

SAVE $1.00

on the purchase of TRIPLETS UNDER THE TREE by Kat Cantrell {available Dec. 1, 2015} or any other Harlequin® Desire book.

Redeemable at participating outlets in the U.S. and Canada only. Not redeemable at Barnes & Noble stores. Limit one coupon per customer.

52613164

Canadian Retailers: Harlequin Enterprises Limited will pay the face value of this coupon plus 10.25¢ if submitted by customer for this product only. Any other use constitutes fraud. Coupon is nonassignable. Void if taxed, prohibited or restricted by law. Consumer must pay any government taxes. Void if copied. Millenium1 Promotional Services ("M1P") customers submit coupons and proof of sales to Harlequin Enterprises Limited, P.O. Box 3000, Saint John, NB E2L 4L3, Canada. Non-M1P retailer—for reimbursement submit coupons and proof of sales directly to Harlequin Enterprises Limited, Retail Marketing Department, 225 Duncan Mill Rd., Don Mills, Ontario M3B 3K9, Canada.

U.S. Retailers: Harlequin Enterprises Limited will pay the face value of this coupon plus 8¢ if submitted by customer for this product only. Any other use constitutes fraud. Coupon is nonassignable. Void if taxed, prohibited or restricted by law. Consumer must pay any government taxes. Void if copied. For reimbursement submit coupons and proof of sales directly to Harlequin Enterprises Limited, P.O. Box 880478, El Paso, TX 88588-0478, U.S.A. Cash value 1/100 cents.

5 65373 00076 2 (8100)0 12107

COUPON EXPIRES JAN. 4, 2016

Available wherever books are sold, including most bookstores, supermarkets, drugstores and discount stores.

www.Harlequin.com

® and ™ are trademarks owned and used by the trademark owner and/or its licensee.
© 2015 Harlequin Enterprises Limited

HDCOUP1115